Past Prai

T0119663

for *Acts of Love*
Yearning characterizes these stories, which have the tragic immediacy of bitter quarrels overheard in the night.

—*Publishers Weekly*

Jim McKinley is the best storyteller I know.

—Richard Rhodes

Telling the truth is the writer's hardest task. McKinley is a first-rate writer.

—Janet Burroway

for *The Fickleman Suite*
McKinley delivers wit and insight into the often bewildering conditions of modern life.

—*Studies in Short Fiction*

for *The Woman in the River*
The narrative is rich in period detail and captures especially well the two-sidedness of the late 1940s: the high standard of conduct demanded by respectable society and the hypocrisy and cynicism that kept that society operating.

—*The Kansas City Star*

who
taught me
to
Swim

Also by James McKinley

The Woman in the River
The Fickleman Suite
Acts of Love
Assassination in America

who
taught me
to
Swim

New & Selected Stories

James McKinley

BkMk Press
University of Missouri-Kansas City

BkMk Press
University of Missouri-Kansas City
5101 Rockhill Road
Kansas City, Missouri 64110
(816) 235-2558 (voice)
(816) 235-2611 (fax)
www.umkc.edu/bkmk

Cover art: "The Seal" by James G. Davis
Author photo: Scott Gardner
Cover and interior book design: Susan L. Schurman
Managing Editor: Ben Furnish

BkMk Press wishes to thank Bill Beeson, Teresa Collins, Emily Iorg,
Sandra Meyer, and Chelsea Seguin.

Library of Congress Cataloging-in-Publication Data
McKinley, James
    Who taught me to swim: new and selected stories/ by
James C. McKinley
    p. cm.
Summary: "This book is a collection of fourteen short stories that primarily
feature mid-life American male protagonists in the late 20th and early 21st
centuries dealing with retrospection (particularly over coming of age and
love), marital strain, and the search for fulfillment in life. Settings include
the United States (particularly the Midwest, Kenya, and Spain)"—Provided
by publisher.
    ISBN-13: 978-1-886157-61-3 (pbk.: alk.paper) 1. Middle-aged
men—Fiction.
        I. Title.
    PS3563.C3815 W48 2007
    813/.54 22
                                            2007017316
The author gratefully acknowledges the editors of the following publications where
these stories first were published:
Acts of Love (Breitenbush Books): "Chambers" & "Kitchen Conversation"
The Fickleman Suite and other stories (University of Arkansas Press): "Moriarty's True
Colors," "The Novice Writer Explores Cartography," "House Call," "Memorial Day"
The Woman in the River (Vineyard Press): "House Call"
New Letters: "The Novice Writer Explores Cartography" & "Chipmunks"
Missouri Review: "Food"
Southern California Anthology: "7-10"

This book is set in Adobe Jenson Pro, Baker Signet, and New Berolina MT type.

For my family, my writing students,
and especially GTGW

who taught me to *Swim*

I

Chambers

Pauline was always the strong one as far as I knew. And I knew pretty far, from '47 when I got off that train from the VA in Wichita and first went to Chambers Famous Bar. Coming out of old Union Station in Kansas City, it was about the first thing you saw if you turned toward downtown on Main. Big sign: Chambers Famous Bar. Guys from St. Louis would kid that they thought it was a department store—they got one there called Famous-Barr—but then people from St. Louis like to brag. Nobody could mistake Chambers Famous Bar for a department store. Right next to it was the Main Street Hotel. I never really got much farther than them two places in nearly thirty-five years. The Main Street Hotel was okay back then. Clean and respectable. Politicians used to bring their girls there. Later it got seedy. Changed names, changed owners, but never changed sheets. Girls kept coming and going. Travelers got to have girls, I guess—and politicos. Soldiers, too. I did, long time ago. Sometimes I'd get it free from drunk hookers, or if I didn't have the scratch, old Earl, Pauline's husband, the Chambers of

Chambers Famous Bar, would lend it to me. That is until all the girls got to be black and didn't want nobody like me.

Earl, you know, didn't mind the whores. Said everybody had to use what God gave 'em. Pauline'd give him a sort of stare, but she never called him down in public, far as I saw. Yeah, Chambers Famous Bar was the place to be. Really a kind of home from the time I got off the Iwo Special from the Wichita VA. I always called it the Iwo Special 'cause coming up from Wichita was a bunch of us on it that got shot up on that piece of tropical paradise. I left most of an arm, all of an eye and, the VA doctors said, some of my head there, courtesy of Hirohito's Nips, bless their little kimonos. Earl sure liked us vets. He fixed Chambers up real good after the war. He loved to make signs. Made 'em out of silver and gold paper. He painted dozens, too. "Veterans Welcome," he'd hand up. "Beer, the Best, 10¢. Beer, the Very Best, 15¢." For Pauline's cooking, all kinds of signs. As time went on he made more and more. And he did other things to make Chambers famous.

Like around 1950 when the Santa Fe and the U.P. and the Katy were pouring people into Kansas City faster than Pendergast poured concrete, right then, Earl got a whole orchestra installed in Chambers. Yeah, a whole orchestra. The vote buyers and the girls and the cops and the gandy dancers and hobos and just about everybody who heard about it came to gape and drink the Very Best Beer (politicians always had a shot alongside and the cops drank free). Everybody'd watch and listen. It was a hell of a thing. 'Course us regulars could tell Pauline had two minds about it. She was proud all right that Earl'd gotten it, and she liked the music, but it fretted her that he'd be fool enough to lay out good money just because he wanted us to be happy. 'Least that's what I thought then.

Even so, when that orchestra played, Pauline lit up. Earl would take her out from behind the bar where she was piling boiled eggs or pumicing the grill, and whirl her around amongst the customers on that linoleum until you got dizzy watching.

She just glowed. Earl's orchestra got so famous he made a huge sign for it, a "frieze" some guy called it, that shouted out in big silver letters, "Chambers Famous Bar Band, Known from Coast to Coast." That was pretty near true.

Earl wouldn't ever tell where he got his orchestra. My guess was it came from one of those companies that used to make things for carnivals, back when there were street carnivals, back when nobody was afraid to be in the streets after dark. Old Earl knew carnies. He was something of a magician, like a barroom Houdini. Anyway this orchestra sat up there on Earl's mezzanine, about six feet above the jukebox. There were seven of them, all made of painted pot metal, each one I'd make about ten inches tall, with monkey suits painted on. A leader was in front, waving his baton for all get-out. And a drummer wanging away. The trumpet man and saxophone player and trombone man were all standing up together swaying. The piano player's hands thumped the keys and his head nodded, and the bass-man beat on those metal strings while he nodded, too, how good he was.

See, they were all up on a little stage, and when Earl or somebody put money in the jukebox (it was loaded right up to the end with all the good old stuff—Glenn Miller, Woody Herman, the Dukes of Dixieland, Sinatra, Peggy Lee—all the class acts) this scarlet curtain would pull back, the music would start and there was the orchestra. Looking up there, it was like your world shrank. You'd believe those little metal men were playing their hearts out for you, and everybody in Chambers Famous Bar would be dancing and smiling and kissing and looking up at them. Lately I think how cuckoo we was, but we always had a good time at Chambers. Like time and your troubles had stopped. Earl kept his orchestra playing, even when times changed and the neighborhood ran itself down. Sure, then you'd get brown-bag boozers in for their muscie who'd spit up at it, or Indians and blacks and Orientals who'd want to know how come all the players were white.

"They just are," Earl'd say. "Just made that way. But the music's good ain't it? And that's Ellington playin'."

Earl'd wink at me—I spent most of my time there in those days on the far corner stool, nursing my disability beers—and Pauline would shake her head. Sometimes she'd have to shoo them boozers out. "Go on, get along, we got work to do," she'd say, but smiling. "Earl'd talk with the Devil if the Devil'd talk back," she'd say, and go back to making the ham salad and counting the hot dogs. They went on that way for years. We got old together, me and Pauline and Earl, 'least our bodies did. Earl used to kid me about that, too. Every New Year's while the orchestra played "Auld Lang Syne" he'd say, "Now, Jack, another year, but you still aren't as old as us. Hell, you don't have as much left to get old." He'd laugh like a banshee and Pauline would scold him and pour me a real California champagne. Earl was a great kidder and a great sport. Customers came in just as much to see him as for the orchestra and the signs and Pauline's chili.

I watched folks come in and spin around Earl and then leave, glad as a Goodyear on old U.S. 66. Earl could play mouth harp and spoons (once he got so jacked up he yanked a spoon clean out of the chili and sprayed two hookers with beans and meat). But his specialty was the violin. With the right crowd, and always for pretty women, he'd put a coin in the box and punch up Glenn Miller or Sinatra or somebody sweet and then haul out his beat-up old fiddle. There they'd be, Sinatra singing "Moonglow" and the orchestra clanking back and forth and Earl waltzing behind the bar, scraping out the melody, his eyes closed and on him a smile wide as a rainbow. Once—it was in the '60s—I was there at the corner when he did that for a couple of skinny, pale hippie girls, you know the kind that bragged about doing a little dope (shoot, we did reefers on Iwo, good stuff from Manila-town) and stuffed carnations in their hair and moved around the country passing out quiff to guys who said "wow" and "far out" and couldn't remember their own names. Let alone the girls'. Well, anyway, Earl put in the coin and he and Sinatra and the orchestra played "High Society" as kind of a joke. The girls didn't get it but they liked the scene, they said, and they told Earl it was all "too much," and they kissed Earl and Pauline and bought a few eggs to take with them on the train to the coast. I recall that real clear because right then things started to change in Chambers Famous Bar, and I suppose everyplace else.

Like, I got steady work for the first time since the war, and not just janitoring or night-watching, or some of the stuff they'd let a one-armed, one-eyed vet do in the fifties. Nope, after that nut killed Jack Kennedy and LBJ got his Great Society geared up, I got me an actual job, helping run the gym afternoons at a new "community center" on the Eastside. Just a run-down old school, really, and most of the people were black, but I didn't mind. If they had folks, even just a mom, the kids were usually okay, real nice. The others, well, they'd come in talking street-smart and shoot baskets and pool. After that they'd go out into them dark streets and meet the pimps and pushers and runners and made men and finally go someplace where rats ran the floor.

Me working, I didn't spend as much time at Chambers, just most evenings. I still stayed in the hotel—I think it was the Elgin then—because it was as much home as anyplace. And Earl and Pauline were as much family as anyone. Not that they lived in the Elgin. No, way back in the thirties when they first came up to KC from the Ozarks, they'd bought a nice old place over on the Paseo, over east, not too far from where my gym was. Those days that was a pretty splashy place to live (Earl got the money selling his daddy's hard-scrabble farm to the Corps of Engineers, who were fixing to build a lake out in the middle of nowhere). But by the sixties the Paseo had all changed, too. The cops called it a combat zone because the bad blacks were always messing people up (usually the good blacks), but that didn't move Earl and Pauline. All the time they were living right in the middle of it. Pauline wouldn't move.

"It's my home," she'd say, "and I'm not letting anyone push me out."

Every night when Chambers Famous Bar closed they'd drive home and into the garage and lock it and open about fifty door locks and shut themselves in. Earl could still look tough, like a mean, white Ozark cracker, and I guess that's part of why nobody bothered them. And they had lots of friends in the neighborhood, blacks and some whites who'd hung in there. I think Earl packed a gun for a few years until Pauline made him stop. She said he'd hurt himself or her before he'd get anybody else. They kept being careful. In the late '60s Earl even started keeping his three antique cars in the garage behind the bar's building. In the seventies he got shed of two, needed the money he said, keeping only a '24 Model A, just like it come off the line. Sundays in good weather he'd come over and get it out and him and me and Pauline would drive around town, honking the bulb-horn he had and watching the necks crane. We'd crank her to start, just for fun. Lots of times Pauline'd fry chicken and we'd have potato salad and bean salad and some of Chambers Very Best in a park. Or we might rattle out into the country. "Pauline," he'd say, "let's sell out and move back out here where we can breathe in peace. We ain't getting any younger." I figured Earl was right, and I said so a time or two. But Pauline wouldn't have it.

"What would we do without Chambers?" she'd ask, knowing that he loved it more than she did. She was right. Earl loved that place, and they stayed put.

Like I said, those '60s kicked off the changes. One thing, new vets started to come in. The weirdest was some of 'em came, like me, off the train from the Wichita VA. But they came, too from the coast and the Gulf, from Leavenworth and Riley and Leonard Wood and Chaffee and Rucker and San Diego, they came from all over, some still whole in their uniforms, and some on their way home or to a hospital in shape like me and worse, and ashamed of it. When they started, boy, Earl pulled out all the stops. Sure, he still did the jokes and the signs. He painted up some big American flags, too, and put them up all over until a kid missing a leg wheeled himself over and tore one down, tears

a'streaming and mouth working like he was trying to spit out
something rotten.

Earl practically wore out the orchestra those days, and the
violin, not to forget Pauline, who hustled up enough chili and
dogs and pizzas and burgers and pulled enough free beers to put
Rockefeller in the poor house. And for these new vets Earl did
a really wonderful crazy thing. Up above the bar, through the
ceiling tiles, he hung half-women in just panties (I know they
were Pauline's). Yeah, half-woman mannequins he'd scrounged
from some display-window salesman. Them GIs loved them,
and they'd always ask Earl, "How much is the whole thing?"
You know, joking on the word. "Not for sale," he'd say, "just for
lookin'." And Pauline would giggle so she'd drop her spoon or
whatever. There was another thing, too, for these vets, and really
for anybody now who found Chambers Famous Bar (believe me,
there weren't as many as before). Earl started doing the magic
tricks he used to do only for a few regulars like me, or out on
the picnics when we'd all get a little tight and hoot like damned
star-struck fools.

You know, I always wondered if he practiced at home on the
Paseo, or if Earl was just kind of a natural genius. He was good,
no doubt about it. Sleight of hand better than you'd ever see
on Ed Sullivan, and a helluva lot better than this faggoty guy
they got now who needs a band and three nearly naked girls to
disappear an elephant or a car. He'd take a napkin and tie a real
tight knot in it (you could pull it yourself) and then he'd give
a little move and pull and then it was, no knot, and instead a
big yellow and red streamer. Or he'd take a coin and knock it
through the bar with you an inch from his hands. The usual
stuff, like eggs out of your ears or coins in your pocket or glasses
going south in a towel, well, he tossed them off like a small beer.
But Earl's specialty for soldiers and pretty gals was the rabbits.

I still don't know how he did that trick. Earl would fetch a
good-sized foam rubber bunny from behind the bar. Big as your
hand. Then he'd show it to you, make you feel it, get to know it.

Talking and joking all the time, that showman's smile over you like a wet shirt. Then he'd take the big rabbit and fold it into your hand, and he'd wrap your fingers around it. Funny how soft Earl's hands were, like he'd never done a hard day's work even if he had. Pauline's were rough, and she used to hold them out from her and say, "They look like my mother's and she worked a farm." Anyway, you had the rabbit in your hand, and you damn well knew it, and then Earl would let go your hand and knock on the bar three times and everybody watching would lean forward and stare at your hand.

"Now open it," Earl'd say.

You did, and there they were. Seven little foam rubber rabbits, each different-colored from the big momma rabbit, just laying in your hand like, well, like Creation itself had laid 'em there for you to love. Everybody'd clap then, and the vet would shake his head or the woman would lean across and kiss Earl, and Pauline would set up the bar. The rabbits never didn't work, but you had to see it. The kids at the community center, you know, wouldn't believe it when I'd tell them. "Ain't no magic, for sure, that's just shuck," they said, except for a few that had voodoo or Baptist upbringing.

The first robbery, Pauline said, was like a joke. It was in the early '70s or late '60s, I can't remember which. In broad daylight. Some Bible-blasted ridge runner in from some shit-heel crossroad, pushes his way through the new aluminum door with Earl's Day-Glo sign on it saying "We Support Our Police," and he orders a Best Beer (they were 25¢ by then). So Pauline draws it and brings it over, and the kid says, "I got no money." Earl, now, was at the end of the bar, fussing with a new Hamm's sign, one of them that looked like it had Crayolas melting inside it. When he hears the kid he breaks into his big welcome smile and says, "That's OK, son, it's on us." Then this ridge runner snarls and knocks over his glass and says, "Goddam straight it is, old man, clean out the register," and he pulls out a little bitty knife like you see old Ben Franklin sharpening his pen with in the Budweiser bar posters, and he waves it at Pauline. She recalled she just stood stock-still while the kid's eyes rolled around the place—nobody else in just then—and she heard Earl laugh and watched him come toward the kid, tying a knot in his bar towel. Well, the kid begun to panic and slash the air, so while Earl is telling the kid about how he didn't want to do this and there were places, like the Salvation Army, all time fixing up his knot trick, old Pauline reaches in the register and grabs a fiver and flips it to the kid.

"You know," she told me, "he looked at that money like it was the Devil, and then he grabbed it and ran out the door. I recall he looked back. Can't forget those eyes. They were like the ones on those poor boys who'd been in the Indychina, all hollow and black, like somebody had burned out what was behind them."

Earl figured it simpler. Just somebody down on his luck, he said. That's what he said the first time anyway. I was there for the next, and he felt different after that. It was some years later. Really, I speculated why with all the kooks around in the '70s Chambers Famous Bar didn't have more stick-ups. Probably was because of the cops, for one. The uniforms'd come in pretty regular, and you'd never know if the bum next to you was undercover vice or narking or what, not the way they hung around joints like the Elgin (it may have been the Paragon by then, and it was so bad, so dirty, and with so many nasty hookers and dope dealers that I would've moved if it hadn't been for Chambers). Another thing I think was Earl and Pauline themselves and the way the place looked. It was getting a little raggedy, too, if you know what I mean, and Earl and Pauline were all spotted and knotted with big blue veins, and Pauline had wrinkles inside wrinkles. Both had shrunk and were gray-haired. Me, too, but I wasn't in the public eye. Earl and Pauline, handing out boiled eggs in Coors ashtrays and popping Polish sausages in the new microwave, they just kind of looked pitiful, too old to bother with. Maybe some natural kind of feeling held off some of the badness, I don't know. It sure didn't the time I was there.

It was night, just before closing (Earl had taken to shutting up around nine, just being cautious) and in came black trouble. By then I surely knew it when I saw it—some of my kids just reeked evil-doing and others just the opposite. This dude was wired, you could tell, and I started for the phone near my perch. But he was too quick. He pulls out this shiny piece like General Patton had, looks to make sure nobody else is there, and says, "Cool it, lessen you want another arm off." So I stopped. It's funny what fear does.

I was officially brave. My citation says so, for giving up an arm and an eye to toss a grenade at Nips in a bunker. But really I was scared. If I hadn't had something to do then I'd've spoiled my pants. There in Chambers I didn't have nothing to do, and that's the worst kind of scared. I could tell because my stump itched bad under the leather butt of my tweezers. This bad dude turns to Earl and Pauline. They got eyes like pizza pans, 'cause this was bad shit. The dude leans across the bar—he's got frizzy hair and a fat scar on his right cheek—and he grabs Pauline by the dress front and says to Earl, "I want all the money or I waste old momma here."

I was talking about being brave and how sometimes you can't tell it from scared. Well, Earl could. Quick as a flash, like he was doing a trick, he whaps the dude 'cross the head with a beer glass from under the bar. That unfreezes me, and I come at him with my stool. But we were too old and slow. I see it like it was a movie in my head. That shiny gun lashing across Earl's gray head, and then coming for me. I remember it was like when the grenade rolled back at me on Iwo, just a red flash and a feeling like a big shove, no pain at first, and then you're falling, something wet oozing down your cheek. I swear I saw Pauline screaming, too, her mouth a big "O," and the dude there behind the bar pulling money out of the register with one hand and the other swatting at her with Patton's gun. After that it was just cops and the emergency room until the next day or so when I pieced it all together.

Earl and Pauline were in St. Mary's about a week. I got out of the VA in three days. My head felt like a boil that needed sticking. Both of them had concussions and bruises, and Earl got a bad cut on his hand, I guess from the glass. He couldn't do tricks for about two months. Pauline had a nasty gash on her lip but she was hurt more inside. Even when things were back to normal, every time somebody came in Chambers she'd look scared for just a second before the orchestra and the jokes and Earl's tricks and her cooking let her fight it off and be brave. Like I said, she was tough and strong. Just last year, after they started taking afternoon turns running Chambers, she had a drunk Indian sort of try to rob her. But she sweet-talked him and gave him a pint of muscie and pushed the new silent alarm. When the cops called in a bit later they found the Indian stone asleep from the muscie and Pauline standing over him with a baseball bat. Still, she wasn't the same, even if she acted like it.

Things were just different. We didn't have no more Model A rides, and she and Earl talked about closing the place up. It was about the same with me. There wasn't no great demand for one-armed, one-eyed old men. The job at the community center gave out, and there was so many professors on the street that wanted to be night watchmen that I couldn't find work. Nobody seemed to care much. Like the agencies told me, you're old and most folks want a watchman with two eyes. So I had to go out to the vet's home in Lee's Summit. It was clean and nice, no hookers or dealers, and it was dull as dishwater. Took me an hour and a half to get to Chambers by bus (KC's got no way now to move ordinary people around. It's an automobile town). I only got there once or so a week. Usually the place'd be empty, just Earl or Pauline and an odd drunk. Sometimes both of them would be there in the late afternoon. There weren't any trains anymore so they had none of that business. The wars were all over. The cops had the whores and dealers moved out east. Things were as dead there as at the home. Near to the last time I was there I remember Earl saying he wished they'd sold out years ago and gone back to the country.

"If wishes were horses, beggars would ride," Pauline said. "We just have to do what we have to do." So they stayed living on the Paseo and running Chambers Famous Bar until last year when they finally got too old and tired to keep the place open. Pauline called me at the home.

"Jack," she said, "you ought to know we're shutting up Chambers Friday."

I went to the last day, of course. The orchestra played and Pauline served up free Polishes and beer and Earl did his tricks for some nice younger people who come in by accident from Hallmark Cards, over here by the hulk of Union Station. With them there it was like old times for a bit, dancing and singing and joking and kissing. Some of the old cops came, even the one who'd caught the bad dude what had pistol-whipped us. Some of the other old-timers showed. Funniest were a couple of whores who'd married Southside stockbrokers and gotten real respectable (one looked at me and put a finger 'cross her mouth 'cause her old man was there, looking like he smelled something bad—in the old days it might've been her). It was sad. Glenn Miller could break your heart in the best of times. I was sort of glad I had to catch the bus early. Pauline kissed me goodbye with her old leathery lips and wished me luck. Earl shook my meat hand and said, "You come visit, we'll go for rides." Then he took an egg out of my ear and we both laughed hard for a minute.

I didn't come visit. It was too far, and to tell the truth I wasn't feeling too good either. A guy here said once you've shot up the body it knows it and one day it'll take its revenge. I guess so. Or maybe it was just years. Whatever, not long after Chambers closed I was in and sometimes out of a chair with something circulatory, and trying like hell to stay in the home and out of the VA hospital, so I never made it to the Paseo. I heard from Earl once. He was still jaunty, calling to say Chambers Famous Bar had been bought by a real operator who was turning it into a real classy place, meaning a wood-and-ferns cocktail bar for the Hallmark crowd. I asked about the orchestra and Earl said they'd just ripped it out and smashed it, but that he couldn't have done anything, he'd sold the place lock, stock, and barrel. He said he'd also sold his old Chevy and the Model A to get a new Honda, and that he and Pauline were doing fine, thinking about going to Florida or Arizona or maybe that retirement community on the lake in the Ozarks. Maybe grow a few tomatoes, he joked. Then Pauline come on to say she loved me, and one day they'd come out to see me, and that things were okay.

That was the last I heard until I read in the *Star* yesterday that Earl and Pauline Chambers, former tavern operators, had been knifed to death in their home on the Paseo by some teenage youths who'd kicked in the basement door. It said robbery was the apparent motive and the police had two suspects in custody. Services were pending.

I know the guys at the home wondered why the hell I was crying in the newspaper. Hell, I'd seen lots of friends dead, ugly-dead, in pieces. But a picture popped into my head. I saw it real clear. I saw Earl and Pauline in their kitchen, laughing and talking about Chambers' old times and about the Ozarks and Florida. Earl is drying the dishes and Pauline is washing. There's orchestra music on the radio, golden oldies, and Earl is whistling and doing a little waltz-shuffle while he dries. Then there's a chill, like somebody opened a beer cooler, and here're the kids, sweating and grinning out of being scared and sliding into the kitchen with them ten-dollar knives open in their hands like it was a kind of war.

And I see Pauline's eyes come up to meet theirs, and they blink and she don't, and her hands come out of the water to make fists. Earl stops whistling and waltzing and starts to tie a magic knot in the towel. He takes a step toward them, a joke in his mouth. Pauline screams when the knives start, not because she's scared, but because of Earl and me and Chambers Famous Bar and the old days. Last I see, real clear, Earl's hand twitching as he falls, like no matter what he'd still make the momma bunny have babies and things would go on forever.

Food

G rist for the mill, he decided. Food for thought. Or maybe
it all was thought, meditation, the torturing examining-
the-life process all the wise ones prattled about. But why every
midnight? Why did he awaken himself from the cobwebbed
conversations and disconnected scenes of his anxious dreams to
slide up on his elbows and stare at his sleeping, lovely wife and
wonder how he had come to feel completely hollow? Or maybe,
really, sort of famished. For soul food, maybe.

Gingerly, he swung to put his feet on the number-one oak
flooring, then into his Kmart slippers. When he stood, the old
brass bed, its mattress resting on green-painted springs, groaned,
creaked, bounced. His wife's breathing stayed steady. He moved
through the doorway, then took the right into the bathroom.
He urinated as quietly as possible, directing his stream to the
sides of the bowl. Was the stream as powerful as in the past?
Was his prostate going? He noted with disgust the swell of his
belly. Hardly looked like he was starving. Then, reluctantly as
he had for the past two decades, he looked at the mirror. That
face! The droop of jowls, the twenty tiny scars from various auto

accidents, the lines coursing the dark sacs beneath his eyes, but at least those were still blue, still clear. Yet how could that be he, Paul Pastor, he who in the full burst of youth had set out forty years ago to eat the world that was his oyster? He for whom opportunity was merely a menu from which he would order what he would? Surely not, yet inevitably, yes. Looking down at the sink, he brushed his capped teeth carefully, thoroughly, then padded out to the kitchen.

Twelve-forty-seven, the clock said. Paul remembered his mother, now long dead, had told him that was the hour he was born, so here he was, seeking to feed the inner man with bread and milk, as he'd done when a child, and she was maggot food. The world's ways worked mysteriously indeed, except at the simplest level when everything became something else's meal, sooner or later. The refrigerator's light comforted him, so dependable, so neutral. So did the skim milk's light, thin taste suffusing the coarse wheat bread he dipped into it. Must keep those arteries clear so the maggots must wait long for him. He carried his glass to the butcher-block table. Well, it wasn't really butcher-block. No animals had been dismembered on it for consumption in elaborate sauces that tried to conceal the basic carnivore transaction between humans and other species. Not that vegetarians offered any special contrast. Who was to say a rutabaga didn't feel, didn't have a soul? And in the end, the animal and the vegetable both wound up as sewage, so what was the point of discriminating? What was any point of anything?

Paul finished his snack. He didn't feel soothed or drowsy. In fact, he felt jumpy, as if he were a plucked string. Jumpy and still hollow. Time again, he sighed, to review, to try to find cause and effect, to locate where, when, why he'd gone off the tracks, unloaded his inherent worth, become an unfilled boxcar on some lost siding. He knew from past reviews that he'd never find what he sought, and that the examining-the-life exercise went at the speed of light, little cuttings of memories flashing on his interior screen so quickly that when he tried to stop one and fathom, poke, explore it, the very process provoked another cutting. And so on. Nevertheless, Paul had an organizing method, and he knew he must persevere. At least he'd get sleepy doing this.

First category: career. These snippets so familiar, so easy to examine. Middle. That was Paul Pastor. Middly. Middling. He saw himself in grade school. Well-scrubbed, frightened to politeness by loving, cold parents and parish priests. Always wanting to please. Trying not, in his father's phrase, to get his bowels in an uproar. Trying hard at his tasks, succeeding at the excellent but not the superior level. Patrol boy. Piano lessons. Organized baseball and football, unorganized hockey, biking, admiring girls and their mysterious growth, fearing his own. Photos of his parents and their only child at his grade-school graduation, everyone smiling, Paul's hair slicked back, his smile smarmy, desperate. That summer he caught a foul ball hit by Luke Appling, and the famous shortstop signed it. Paul had never been happier. Then on to high school where he played J-V baseball, served as secretary of the student council, was class treasurer, earned Bs, learned how to neck, to grope, to deceive in sexual matters, but never lost his cherry. Proms, exams drifted by, the former with fairly pretty, fairly popular girls, the latter addressed earnestly but never brilliantly. Good enough by plenty to get him into the state university, where he did pretty much what he'd done in high school except at a more frenetic pace. His sophomore year he got laid by his fraternity's most notorious punch, and his mother died. Ever since, Paul had mused on the link between sex and death. His junior year he started dating the girl he married after graduation. She was a virgin on their wedding night. He graduated with a 3.2 GPA and since times were good, got a "distribution" job, meaning sales. Here Paul's middleness paid off, he figured. Buyers of anything were cautious folk, and his style fit them. Through booms and recessions Paul had work while his wife had three children, now all grown and as distant as his father, who resided in a nursing home on the West Coast, sequestered by Paul's stepmother, twenty years his father's junior. Now, four years from retirement, Paul was an upper-middle in class, in his work. He first-named only close associates and clients, and the only famous man he'd known was his company's CEO, who came to speak at the semi-annual sales meetings. He was respected, he felt, even liked by his colleagues and friends and, he supposed, his children. Feared by no one. Loved, he guessed, by his wife. Himself loving his wife and kids in a general, fluorescent way, without heat, as if he were a firefly in a bottle. His career, that run through life's external hoops and hurdles, he'd nearly completed. His company, the nation's fifth largest, would give him a retirement party and exhale happily since Paul's departure would fit right in with downsizing. He'd have ample pension and social security and his prudent investments to live on in a middle-class manner. He'd have his wife and family. All that was prescribed as desirable. Mediocritas. Neither feast nor famine. Yet here he sat in his kitchen feeling there was nothing in the fridge or pantry that would make him feel less empty, less hungry.

Second category: life. Paul had to smile at this snippet. Hell, he'd tried to feed on life, so there was a bit of hypocrisy in the flitting scenes of his career. He'd surely edited that category so the self-examination wouldn't be damaging. But life, well, some of those scenes showed him famished. Paul picked up his milk glass, curled his hand tightly around it. The women on his sales swings, what a cliché, and not too many of them. Maybe eight. With them, well, he'd felt fuller, at least in bed. When he came, and they did, or pretended to, he felt in touch with something that satisfied the gnawing in his belly. Original sin, maybe, or original creation. Union, participation in and with another, as when enzymes broke down his bread and milk into constituent molecules that swirled together in a gastric stew that couldn't be too different, could it, from the gaseous soup ignited by the big bang? They'd been nice women, too, lonely as he was, and no whores among them. Professional women, or good-hearted housewives as starved as he was. Not one had ever demanded more than good meals, some entertainment, and sex. Perhaps that was because he was a good salesman, but still. Yes, a kind of satisfaction, but it always passed when they left, or he did. The only things close to that full feeling had been when his children had been infants and he'd held them close, felt their softness, smelled the powder and oil, and imagined their innocence. And when a child had succeeded at something, his one son at football, his daughter at the flute, his other son in debate. And, he admitted, sometimes in the long evenings when he and his wife sat alone, not speaking, but in different ways assessing themselves, telling themselves how lucky they had been, touching familiar household items—a photo here, a pottery piece there—as talismans, sensible objects that might make them in their nest less empty. And they had been good parents, he'd been a good father, loving the children, clothing them, feeding them. What else is life? Sure, short-term business deals and the bonuses. Some memorable golf rounds. Funerals, more lately from his in-laws' side. Vacations, to Europe twice, to Mexico, to the West, East, South, although if it weren't for the snapshots he wouldn't remember much except a few meals and the way the weather was. His wife wanted to go to Alaska on a cruise, the food was so wonderful everyone said, and they could go ashore and look at animals. Paul didn't care, and that was just the problem. Here he was highballing down toward his last stop, and he just didn't fucking care! Didn't care about any of it right now, least of all sharing a cabin on a ship with a wife who'd become an icon, a statue in the chapel of his life, and with about as much flesh-and-blood relevance. Paul looked at his hand. The knuckles and fingers white except for a few brown age spots. He wished he could break the glass so he could clean up his cuts, but he wasn't strong enough. He unclasped and put the glass down. Maybe a cookie would help. He fetched an Oreo from the cupboard, pried it in two and licked the cream off before crunching the top side.

So, the final category: dreams. What constituted his ration of those? He had them, certainly, big and small. In an actual dream, although not the one that had awakened him tonight, Paul saw himself as a submarine creature, finning through azure clear water, skirting rocks, reefs, tube worms, anemones, playing with other creatures as strangely shaped as he. In that dream, Paul possessed an enormous head dominated by globular eyes that could see in every direction, so that when he spied what might be a predator he flicked his powerful body away at flank speed. Oddly, he fed on a mysterious powder that descended to him from somewhere above the surface, for when he skimmed the surface there shone only more blue and a hot, incandescent light. His only discomfort in the submarine world came when he defecated a long string that refused for some time to depart his anus, so that he swam in perfect freedom trailing a strand of shit. Yet eventually, it fell off.

Of more concrete dreams, that is the plan-dreams wherein Paul considered what to do when he no longer had to sell, no longer was a bottom feeder, two most provisioned him. The first, he recognized, could devour him if realized, and it required perhaps more than he could do. Simply put, he'd somehow fill himself with activities, causes, self-help manuals and support groups, even church, until he felt satiated to bursting. He'd act out loving his wife until he again loved her as he once had. Even though he'd never admitted his infidelities, he knew she knew, had for ten years. He could date it with precision because that's when they lost their appetites for one another, had begun to tell petty lies about nearly everything from shopping to news from the kids, as if daily to prove their mutual distrust. But trust and desire could be nourished, he'd read, by pretending them, by programming yourself, and what better time than during retirement—particularly with all the activities. Maybe, just maybe, he could make this plan-dream number-one work.

Paul squirmed in his chair to help conjure plan-dream number two. He heard his stomach grumble, and it was only 2:05, a long way from his breakfast granola and yogurt. He filled his milk glass again, then resumed his post at the table. Number two. He sighed so deeply his milk swirled. If any dream was impossible, this one qualified. But there'd been one woman once, out in Bozeman, who'd said as she dressed, "your heart's hungry, you'd better feed it." He'd contested that, he remembered, saying he had a rich, full life, really. And she'd said, "sure, that's why we're here together. Look, feed it or be fodder for others." Then she'd just left, just walked out, and though he searched the bars and lounges, revisited the restaurant where they'd eaten, he'd never found her. Yet he remembered. Remembered that exchange, remembered the full moon silvering the mountains, remembered the sharp air, the slapping of a running river, the confluence of place and event with a hope that prickled his neck hairs, with the pure release of shared orgasm. Plan-dream number two was, blindly, on faith and with hope, to seek all that again. Alone. But even as he dreamed that he felt fear creep on him, kitchen-cold, and guilt, too, eating at him.

Paul stood and shook, like a dog fresh from a bath. To hell with all this. Two-thirty now, and he had to get up, eat, digest his meals and his paperwork and what life served him, wife and kids included. He snapped off the light, then felt his way back to the bedroom. He heard his mate's steady breathing, so familiar he could have used it to retrieve more snippets, but he was through with that for tonight. Best just to rest, let things be, not cook up anything new for now. He lowered himself onto the mattress, trying not to bounce the springs or squeak them. He patted his stomach. Full enough, yet he felt hungry. Then, completely unbidden, a line of poetry came to him: "there is some shit I will not eat." And Paul sat straight up again.

Kitchen Conversation

My wife is crying and telling me about her lover again. She has had only two, many years apart. I have had many, so I listen with the hypocrite's courtesy. She tells again how first he wants her and then he doesn't and how she feels unwanted by him and now by me, because she knows I love someone else, and what is there left for her?

"I'm still living here," I say.

"It doesn't matter if you don't want to," she says, and sniffles. Truthfully, I don't want to. But I don't not want to, either.

"You've never wanted anything," my wife says, and bursts into a full cascade of tears. Even today her acuteness sometimes comes like those lightning flashes back in the '60s. I was young then and lay awake for hours after our dates, nursing a hard-on, and being struck by a bolt convincing me she was the smartest, prettiest girl in our part of the world. Now, though, we're both wrong. I have wanted something, but never known what.

"What do you want?" I ask. Her answer bubbles toward me like lava.

"I want to go away with him and live together."

Suddenly I want to make love to her, but she is not with me.

"But he's a foreigner," I say. "He has to go back to Transylvania or wherever."

"He is your friend," she says. "Don't be cruel. Or stupid. You seduced his wife."

"Is that why he's fucking you?" I ask. And then I am sorrier than I have been for a long time. I have shot animals whose eyes have looked like hers do. She starts heaving like she's seasick.

"I'm sorry," I say. I know all this is only because we are both hurt, she explicably and me inexplicably.

"Would you like another drink?" I ask.

"Yes," she says, drying her eyes. "I'm drinking too much, aren't I?"

The highballs are a habit, not easily broken. Brown bourbon goes over ice. I think about her lover. He, too, is brown and Baltic cold. She is bound for trouble, and I can't stop her. We had a friend once whose cherished son got drunk for the only time in his life and lay down stuporish on a railroad track just in time for the 2:05 A.M. express. It's like that.

"He makes me happy," she says. He doesn't, I think, which is why she is about to cry again.

"And I don't?"

"You did," she says. "And you try." She drinks, then stares into her bourbon. The kitchen clock, malfunctioning these past few years, whines as if it cannot go on. I wonder where time goes.

"How did this happen?" she asks, in a voice meant for childbirth.

She means how did she fall in bad love again, and I have no answer. "How" is a word for noble savages. Awkwardly I pat her shoulder. She softens, quiets. We know the gesture comes of manners and long habit. We know he will not go away with her. Standing with my hand on her shoulder, feeling her breathe, I suddenly think of a baby I read about, who was born with an incurable heart defect. They put a baboon's heart in her. I think, if she lives and grows to mating age she will be our sister, beastly where we should be human.

"You know I love you, too," she says finally.

"I know."

"It's only that I love him so much, and I've had so little."

"So little love?"

She nods. Now I am the wounded animal. I don't know what to do. We could embrace. Kiss. Maybe make old, familiar, imitation-love. We could. But we will not. We stay, she sitting, trembling only a little, and my hand is on her shoulder. The kitchen clock whines. Outside a few cicadas sing. An ice cube falls from the top of its pile to the bottom of a highball glass. Then I think what it is I want.

"Do you remember schmoos?" I ask.

She looks up. The tear-streaks meander across her cheeks leaving chalky trails from the pouched eyes. He is much younger than she.

"Al Capp's schmoos?" she asks. She smiles. "The little white animals?"

"They tasted like pork or fried chicken. They lived to serve. They followed Little Abner and Daisy Mae around trying to make them happy. They were good-hearted and always happy, even when being eaten alive. Do you remember?"

"Yes," she says.

I squeeze her shoulder and feel her recoil, shrink into some faraway place.

"I want to be back when there were schmoos," I say. "I'd like to be schmoo-hearted." She weeps then and does not stop until I slap her. After that we're both quiet for a long time, until the bruised sky lets go its last red streaks, and we're in the darkening kitchen alone, my hand on her, listening to the clock whine and the ice turn into water.

II

Moriarty's True Colors

Moriarty pressed his nose against the storm door's glass. He kept his hips slightly thrust back so his Levis wouldn't touch the panes and cool his erection. Next to him, standing on small white hind feet, was Louie, their black-and-white cat. Louie, too, stared out at the gray, rainy morning. Across the street, crouched beneath a bush, his lady friend moaned. Louie's erection, if he had one, was hidden up in his body. On Moriarty's other side stood Tashi. Moriarty believed Tashi was the horniest Lhasa apso in America, and certainly one of the biggest. Low groans issued from his bearded visage, like temple chants. Tashi lusted for his mother, a block away, just into heat again. The dog's testicles bulged under long, silky black fur. Moriarty wondered if his fellow lusters felt as ignoble as he, but of course they did not. They didn't have to admit animality. They were animals.

"Still raining?" Moriarty's wife asked.

"Yes."

He heard Sarah's pen return to the letter. A love letter. Last winter's lover, now far away. Moriarty's excitement subsided. He'd not get out this afternoon, not find his love, his lover.

"Meeeeee-owwwww," moaned Louis.

Tashi growled, uttered a stifled little bark.

"Oh, God! Those animals!" his wife said. "Just let them out. With any luck they'll be run over."

Moriarty turned from the door. His right foot thrust Louie back. A hard look drove Tashi back toward the kitchen table.

"They're just horny," he said. She threw cold eyes, then scratched out a phrase. He sat at the table. They were comfortable enough with one another now. They'd reached that penultimate stage at which they still loved one another, but didn't like one another. He watched her pen form the blue words. Once he had vowed never to write love letters. Say it with flowers, say it with drink, but never, never say it with ink. Something perverse happened, though. Now he could write love letters much easier than love.

"Where did we go wrong?" Moriarty asked. Louie leaped onto the chair beside him, mewling. He pushed him off. The cat's paws thumped the worn linoleum.

"We? You started it."

"No," he said. "You started it. I just continued it. In between Victor and what's his name."

She scratched out another phrase. A draft. She would perfect it.

"Between Victor and Franz were fifteen years," she said. "And *three kids* and you."

Tashi sidled up to rest his head on Moriarty's lap. Fair enough. He knew his wife could add: *and your several conquests.*

"Abstinence makes the heart grow fonder?"

She managed a smile.

"I didn't abstain from you. Did you abstain from anybody, fond of them or not?"

"Love's different, right? Now you're in love."

"Yes. Aren't you?"

He didn't know.

"Aren't you? Or has it all been some time-release revenge?" She held the pen between her hands as if she would break it.

"I still love you," he said. It felt half-true, like a promise to a wheedling child.

She looked again at the paper. A thin howl came from outside. Tashi's head swiveled toward the door. Louie stood there again, against the glass, head cocked. Tashi moved toward the cat. The pen moved again. Moriarty felt each stroke.

"Do you love him?" he asked. "Actually love him?"

"I think so."

"Is that what you're writing?"

"Part of it. He's thousands of miles away." Tashi sniffed Louie. The cat showed teeth when Tashi tried to mount him. A hiss, a quick box to the snout, and the dog was off. Safe for now, Louie darted for his pillow.

"Animals," he said.

"What's the difference?" she asked.

"I still love you. I do. Only we're different. Everything is."

"You're thinking about the baby, aren't you?"

Now Tashi pawed at the door, claws rasping on the glass. Moriarty saw that sunlight had come to play on the rain, painting the drops yellow as lemons. Moriarty thought he could see another color in the canine skull, a pulsating red glow. Instinct's color? What then was reason's color? The humanizing color? But wasn't instinct also human? Maybe all the somatic, genetic, experiential essences were colorless. If so, then what color was he? Or she? Tashi, discouraged, dropped to lie on the entrance mat.

"Aren't you?" she said again.

"Yes. It started to get different then."

She looked again at the letter. Her pen stabbed an *i*'s dot. Inside her skull would be what color, he wondered. Anger's orange? Sorrow's bruise-purple? Something pastel, maybe, between love and hate. Love and hate for him, for them, for herself, for perhaps, even the baby now become a fine son.

"I'm sorry," he said.

"I'm not." The pen came up to point at Moriarty's eyes. "Look at him. Really look, like when he comes off the bus. He's splendid. Like a little god."

"Funny, that's what the Mexicans called the magic mushroom."

She stared through him.

"Don't be cynical. He's healthy."

"I meant it," Moriarty said. "He's magic, too."

She returned the pen to the paper. The scratching irritated Moriarty's ears. He remembered his shock when she told him there would be another. Do you want it? Yes. Are you sure? It's alive, it's mine. His shrug. His nine-month, white-red resentment. Then the summer solstice, the baby lying sideways, emergency surgery during a thunderstorm that cut the electricity, a boy baby born in generator light when the sun was at the full. Now he loved the boy, but she loved him more. Moriarty hoped it was enough to fill her where her lover had been, where he had once been.

"Why?" he asked. "Why did you have him?"

She held the pen again like a stick to be broken.

"Which?" she asked. "Doesn't matter, does it?"

Moriarty turned to see the sunlight and prismatic rain drops.

"To keep you," she said then. "Because I loved you. An old trick that lost its magic." She laid the pen on her letter. He could feel her slowed respiration. He could feel her glowing amber like the afternoon light.

"Yes," he said. He thought, now my son cries when anything, a plastic soldier, is hurt.

"Yes," he said again.

She stood, holding her letter and pen.

"I'm going to lie down."

Her passing disturbed Louie. The cat stretched, pushed his paws out like furry quatrefoils. Louie arched his way to stand beside Tashi, who roused himself. Cat and dog, they stood to stare out. A lemon drop snailing down the door caught the cat's eye. He mewled. The bearded dog groaned, high and strangled. The cat's tail switched, its end curled like a field-hockey stick. Moriarty sighed and went to stand between them.

The light seemed to flow in the rain, to coat the basketball goal, driveway, street, horizon. Soon the child, his son, would step from the bus into the golden puddles. Perhaps he, too, would glow, perhaps roseate. Soon it would be solstice time again. Heat time. Peasants would throw tokens of their troubles into bonfires, eat magic mushrooms, take the little god into themselves to conceive visions of what's beyond: reds, blues, yellows, oranges, purples, all twirly cornucopias melding the spectrum of perception. So, what color would Moriarty and Sarah glow? Animal and human? Old and young?

Moriarty pulled hard on the door handle.

"Go on," he said. "Go!"

Tashi bounded through, his tail up, water and light shedding from his fur. Louie darted like a leopard cleaving soaked Serengeti saw grass. Moriarty watched them dash their separate ways to love, splashing across the street along different paths.

Then he turned, irrationally aroused, and started for the bedroom, which he recalled she had done all in white, very long ago.

Moriarty's Place

M oriarty, adrift and bereft, didn't adore his resting place. He only knew it seemed for the moment more peaceful than any dwelling he'd shared with any of his women, and certainly calmer than the Masses he disrupted when he had a spell and shouted obscenities. Actually, his spells now seemed to be in remission, and maybe that was due to this place. Not that it had any obviously therapeutic qualities, other than being painted white so it resembled the monk's cells he'd often imagined would be heaven if only he could disentangle himself from the things of this world like sex, money, guilt, remorse, even joy and ecstasy. A real monk's cell, he'd imagined, would be a cool, white center, the Nirvana reached through satori, where he would be beyond desire, beyond sorrow, beyond the veil of Maya. What Thomas Merton had, Moriarty thought, until he remembered that Merton had been electrocuted by an electric fan cord in Thailand. Ignominious. Igmonkish. Unless it had been the Electric Age's version of God's bolt from the blue. Ezekiel's ride.

In his place, of course, Moriarty took care not to step on any electrical cords, which were unnecessary anyway since although the building dated to the 1950s it did have ample wiring inside the walls. He also had lots more than did Merton in his old Kentucky home, the Trappist monastery. Moriarty had life to observe and a windowed kitchen three times the length and twice the width of a grave. And a telephone which, so far as Moriarty knew, was not standard issue even in Mary Baker Eddy's Boston tomb. Moriarty often wondered whom the founder of Christian Science might call if she revived and found a phone. Pizza Hut? American Airlines? Damon's Construction and Excavating? Or worst, a physician. Moriarty also had memories of Sandra here, and photographs of Sarah and their children, and a physical reminder of his last wife, Kimberly, through a VitaMixer she'd brought and left by his newly acquired old Ford Escort. He had the bedroom with brown water stains beneath the sill and the remnants of the previous monk's tenure in pieces of transparent tape on the walls. Posters? Certainly, but of what, of whom? Moriarty imagined they could have been U2 or Enya, but it could as well have been an image of Perry Como. It didn't matter. He also had a bathroom with a shower, and a living/sitting room, also with stains beneath the sills, that he'd furnished with castoffs from prior dwellings, purchases from the Salvation Army store, and odd pieces scrounged from the piles of goods this transient society left at the curb. He was especially fond of a Buddhist house shrine he'd found while walking in what the local bigots called "the yellow neighborhood." The bus driver, a black man, hadn't given it a second look when Moriarty boarded with it, but a gnarled white man, in a World War II army officer's overcoat, pockets bulging with brown-paper-wrapped bottles, snarled that he'd "flame-throwed lots of little yellow fuckers in front of those things." Moriarty installed the shrine in front of the living-room windows as his meditation station, and dedicated it to Merton.

One of Moriarty's neighbors was "a little yellow fucker," tall and elegantly slim, her skin the color of cappuccino, her waist narrow enough to be circled by a large golden earring, her modest hips and breasts swelling like hills from the Plain of Jars.

Unfortunately, she was locked in vice to a splotchy-faced Eastern European woman with a street-vendor's voice, who hollered at Moriarty "you vill please separate das recyclables" every time he approached the dumpster.

Of his other neighbors, Moriarty purposefully knew little, although he observed them from his kitchen windows. In all his dwellings, with Sarah, Sandra, Kimberly, in married suburban houses, hotels and urban condos, he'd never sincerely wondered about other people. He'd seen them, but they'd been mere props in the play of his own ego, Merton would say. Now, though, in his medium-sized town in a landlocked state, he *watched* others. Watched them watch the mailbox for money from social security, banks, and savings accounts. Watched them at the welfare office, at the grocery, in the nearby public park, on their stairwells and in the parking lot upon which his kitchen window opened. He saw that those living around him were as untouched by his presence as he was untouched by theirs.

A constant in his observations was a small, bald man whose gait reminded Moriarty of a bantam rooster. Each morning at seven the man crossed beneath Moriarty's window and strode with jerky leg and head bob toward the hospital a block away. An hour later, precisely, he bobbed back. Moriarty pondered this mission. Cancer therapy? Psychiatric counseling? Cardiac rehabilitation? And why did the man live here? Maybe he visited a bedfast relative. Moriarty pictured an Alzheimered wife, drooling, the man squeezing her hand, feeding her, speaking to her of the past, promising a future. But for only an hour a day?

Mysterious, too, was a large black man who sat for hours in his 1976 Impala, staring up at the amber streetlight. And the East Indian-looking man who walked down the block to the hospital in a bloodstained lab coat and came home in a clean one. And the angular, bearded boy who walked a Bouvier de Flandres each morning, the huge bluish dog tugging him along, eventually up the stairs to the boy's apartment, which Moriarty knew was the mirror image of Moriarty's spare space.

Moriarty wondered how they coexisted here without mate or matin. There was a large man whose good car and clothes contradicted his modest living; a tall woman with Florida license plates, who exuded bitterness through her fading tan; a woman in her fifties received a man (former husband?) who came to visit bearing trinkets and his arm in a sling. He coached football, the woman told Moriarty at the dumpster.

Not all the stories he watched were strange or sad. He observed a matched pair of tall blond male homosexuals happier and fonder with each other than Moriarty and any of his women had ever been, right down to the parting kiss of a morning. A duet of women, too, seemed happy, although one stood willowy, lithe as a gazelle, gorgeous in her bottomland-black skin, while the other stood short and stocky, pale as cirrus clouds, her frank face open as a great plain. Moriarty observed other life forms, too. He watched birds—jays, mourning doves, sparrows, robins, grackles, the occasional brown thrush—in the trees behind the building's parking lot. Squirrels, too, worked the trees, and a housecat or two, and before the trees and the little houses were leveled by a yellow Caterpillar 973, Moriarty watched an old dog wander the tiny backyard, Edenic with flowers and ornamental shrubs that his old mistress kept for him. Moriarty envied the dog, and for no detectable reason he wept watching, just as he smiled, or even laughed, seeing the squirrels lug the green hulls of black walnuts bigger than their heads across the parking lot and into other trees. But when the Caterpillar came, the squirrels and birds left, and Moriarty felt something of himself go, too, some finger lose its grip on this temporary place he'd found, as if what had been bulldozed were not a few houses and trees but the rain forest of his soul. It made him ache to see the men hose down the cat-tracked raw earth to lay the dust, not to nourish and, when the Cat squirmed like a rapist atop the felled trees, Moriarty decided he truly needed another place.

That resolve got mighty help from the old lady with the dog the next day when she surveyed the wreckage while Moriarty was fumbling for his keys in the dusty parking lot. He felt her before he saw her, a chilling clutch on his hand sending Moriarty's heart into aerobic speed.

"You've got paws," he heard. "Prehistoric. Get to your cave."

Moriarty stared into the crinkled face, felt the old dog against his leg, felt the warm stream soak his pants leg, and then watched the pair shamble off through the pitted lot, now sightseers at what had been their home. Where was their place now? Who cared?

Moriarty studied his hands. Yes, paws. A plain of dark hair on the backs, then tufts below the first knuckles, then the long lateral curve of his four fingers to the long nails. On the other side, the pale palm with its lines—was his lifeline long? broken? forked?—and the obverse curves until his eyes came to the thick pads that marked the ends of the digits. OK, paws. But what cave? What refuge?

Up in his white apartment, changing his trousers, Moriarty plumbed what was left of his brain but could come up with nothing that would fulfill the crone's injunction. Why should he pay attention to anything issuing from the clogged channels of an old brain? But then, he thought maybe the seers of all time had been mentally infirm. Holy Scripture could be the journals of stroke victims. Nostradamus might have been an idiot savant or a schizophrenic who in this time would be living in a box over a heating grate. It was the age of analysis, not illumination. The Buddha would be laughed away into a halfway house for peaceful dissenters. Mohammed put in a rubber room for bloody-minded rabble-rousers. Christ... well, Christ would be given a TV network and kept out of sight by His handlers until money was needed. He had a gift for parable, and nothing sells like a miracle story. Lazarus. Loaves and fishes. Water into wine. His handlers probably would let Christ out to appear in a remarkable remake of *It's a Wonderful Life*. He could do Clarence the angel without a single special effect. But what did that have to do with the old lady's command, Moriarty wondered?

Pondering this, he descended the front staircase, past the water-stained floral wallpaper, to the bank of mailboxes, each three inches by twelve, marking them as relics from a time before direct-mail marketing had swept the forests clean. There he found another injunction, this from his landlords. *Please vacate in two weeks*, it said, *this building is coming down to be replaced by a parking facility.* Moriarty stared at the paper, idly noticing the cheap, dot-matrix printing. So, he was an itinerant, between-vocations, middle-aged man with nothing much in the world except memories and prehistoric paws. Time, he decided, to go again to church.

St. Mary's stood hard by the sluggish, brown river that ran through what was left of the city's core. Moriarty chose it after talking with the bishop's aide, who'd said, "well, if you're looking for something eccentric, outside, well, real Catholicism, try St. Mary's of the River. They're, well, they're from Tralfamadore or somewhere." The church, though, didn't look otherworldly. It stood in red brick, its spire and English ivy standing against the flashcube towers, curtain wall Federalisms and Chippendale-topped office-tower monstrosities like an island of old-fashioned sense in a sea of trend-whipped waves. Entering, Moriarty smelled the old odors: candle wax, furniture polish, incense, dust, and the aroma of emptiness, for truly the place was empty. Moriarty checked his watch. The digits stated 9:00 A.M. When he pushed the day button, Sunday popped up. The bishop's aide, as well as the bulletin board in the entryway, had told him there was a special Mass and Retreat at 9:00 A.M. So here was the church and here was the steeple, but even opened up, where were the people? Moriarty strolled the center aisle toward the altar. It faced the pews, in the new way. A rose window, grimy with center-city effulgents, cast white-yellow-blue-red over the altar, the tabernacle, the Holy Book. Moriarty remembered that he hadn't dipped holy water. He turned toward the entrance when, like a tidal wave, people arrived. They poured through the nave doors with rhythmic tramping punctuated by a faint tinkling from the creature at the head of the pack, who wore the black-and-white checkered mask, fool's cap, breeches, tunic and belled, upturned slippers of a court jester. Moriarty recoiled when the creature reached him.

"What, ho, my friends!" the jester bellowed. "A stranger, and most welcome to our ceremony, too!"

Moriarty felt his hand being pumped, and then he was bouncing among the throng whose members had produced horns, whistles, clackers, so to raise bedlam all around. "God is a jester," proclaimed the creature. "Let us worship Him in all His guises!" Moriarty felt himself rushed in the cacophony of the crowd to the communion rail. He felt bile rise, his heart achieve its aerobic state. This didn't suit his ex-seminarian past at all. He whirled to go, but a large hirsute man, in bib overalls and electric pink undershirt, blocked his way. The man waved a clacker and blew out a paper Pinocchio party favor that tickled Moriarty's cheek. Moriarty squealed, whirled again to the altar seeking sanctuary, hearing the crowd chant, "Take, eat, this is somebody's sacred body." He felt the wafer dissolving on his tongue. Then he was turning in a circle with the others, their hands clasped together. Whirling, the chanting still in the air, Moriarty realized he was no longer thinking, was only dizzily being. He wondered when the whirling would stop, when the chant now transformed from "Take eat, take eat" to a jazzy "We have eaten, praise the giver" would end.

Then, as if someone had pulled a clock's plug, they all stopped. Perspiring, Moriarty looked around the circle. Everyone stood with heads bowed. The jester stood in the center. "Now, Lord," he intoned, "grant us Thy peace as we few set forth for Your Place." The congregants murmured "Amen," then Moriarty was in a swirl of people pushing for the door. He noticed two nuns, one in traditional habit and one resolute in gray business suit and white cowl. A few men were dressed as he was, in jean slacks and jacket. Several women wore Sunday dresses. Three or four teenagers rocked around in Levis and sneakers. One group stood aside. There was the large, overalled man, his florid face partly obscured by a wiry red beard. A boy, thin as a ruler. And a young woman in a white jumper over a blue blouse who took him by the hand in St. Mary's parking lot, staring at him through violet eyes, saying "Are you coming?" For no reason, Moriarty nodded, and still hazy, mounted the steps into the school bus.

By the time the yellow bus pulled off the rural highway onto the gravel road, Moriarty estimated they had been riding about an hour. In that time he'd learned from the girl that she was thirty-two, a former Peace Corps volunteer, a vegetarian and widowed by a FARC bullet in Colombia.

"He was an engineer," she'd said. "Building water projects. They thought he worked for the Army, but he worked for AID. He was also a drunk, and mean. Loved guns, so I guess he got ironic justice."

"I'm sorry," was all Moriarty managed.

"I was angry, " she said. "I don't think we should be supplying anybody's army. We should be out in the world helping people. Sometimes I think of him, good in bed, better at the bars and gun shows. We were married only a year and he was gone most of that."

"So, what do you do? I mean, what do you do now?"

"I taught secondary school. I just quit. This retreat is so I can think and feel what to do."

"Retreat?"

Her violet eyes searched his face.

"Yes, this retreat. Isn't that what you came to St. Mary's for? St. Mary's famous Cosmic Joker retreat?"

"Of course," Moriarty had said. He was thankful that the bus was slowing to a halt, tires crunching gravel, in front of a long, low clapboard building set in a clearing surrounded by leaf-shedding cottonwood and cedar trees. Thankful not least because he had several times studied the seamless face of the girl, the symmetry of eyes, brows, lips, nose. Impure thoughts surfaced, but they vanished in the clamor of disembarking and learning that he was indeed on a retreat, in a Zen-Catholic place called Shanti Vanum, and that he, like five others, had been chosen to stay alone in one of the tiny cabins clustered around the main building. There he was to meditate and pray and at evening meetings talk with others. He was to get clothes and food, from the HQ cabin, split his own firewood, take cold baths, cook his meals if he didn't eat in the common hall, and read. Then, in five days they would celebrate All Hallows' Eve, by which time, the Jester promised, Moriarty's soul would be ready to tell him what to do. The jester was, the girl whispered to Moriarty, a priest named Father Jerry, who further promised the group huddled in the meeting room that they would with luck regain a grip on their true selves. They'd get out of the Maya, back to an Ur-state.

Moriarty looked surreptitiously at his prehistoric paws, remembering some of their good and bad deeds, and then how Tess, for that was her name, had held one of them on their bus ride. Father Jerry dismissed them to their cabins with an odd injunction: "Go," he said, "but don't look out the windows, don't watch the world. Look inside, where your world resides. Peace." Moriarty did as he was told. The seamless days passed. He felt himself content almost to the point of bliss, of no-desire.

On their last day, Moriarty stood at the cabin's window following one of Father Jerry's exercises. He tried to imagine himself blind, as if he had never seen himself and so had no self-image except that generated by the soul or by what others said. Something like what Tiresias or, more importantly, Ray Charles and Stevie Wonder had to do. Moriarty stood staring outward trying to see inward, but as so often happened in his life, he couldn't keep his inner eye where it belonged. His eye and consciousness kept straying to the vegetarian widow Tess, doing her Tai Chi outside in the clearing. He could not keep either his inner or outer consciousness from the rise and fall of her breasts and buttocks. Fortunately for his Ur-soul, others soon joined her. The overalls man, whose name was Earl, lumbered into view and began his movements. Then came the painfully thin teenager, Jim, whose slowly gesturing arms looked like pennants in the wind. The gray-suit nun appeared. In her exercises she looked like an ecclesiastical kickboxer. Last to arrive was a woman usually called Harriet, a stocky, multi-personalitied creature who wore jeans and Pendleton shirts except when she became "Julia," at which time she changed to a flowered pinafore, or "Natasha." Moriarty was thankful her disorder did not permit more personalities. He could keep no more than "Harriet-Julia-Natasha" straight even if each had its own distinctive wardrobe. "Natasha's" was his favorite. She wore red damask culottes and a blue-green flowered babushka.

Moriarty sighed. He issued into the group and began to stretch. How sad that his inner eye seldom saw anything. In fact, Moriarty's conviction that he had scant capacity for introspection had only been strengthened by this retreat. He was a hopeless outlooker, though he hoped the outward look might be a particle beam to another being, across which an exchange might happen, like the famous German bridge where spies were exchanged during the late Cold War. Now, going through the meditative movements, he gazed at Thin Jim in whose blood and cells raged the immunodeficiency virus, planted there by a pint of blood infused after he'd been winged by a cement truck. Moriarty could not imagine that the boy would not always be there, his armature gesturing in order to achieve peace, yet that was the Cosmic Jokester's decision. Jim's early death was his inner reality. That could be a kind of peace, Moriarty supposed, and he prayed for Jim a painless passing. No doubt Tess's flawed husband's passing had been painless. The thump of the FARC 7.62 mm bullet into his skull, perhaps a flash of red, and then the merciful darkness. Another random fly swatted by the Jokester. Perhaps her aura of weltschmerz owed to something else, but it was there, as palpable as perfume.

Moriarty's Zen half-pivot brought his particle beam to Earl. Now there swirled another air altogether. Earl, too, was dying, but of a random swipe so rare, so bizarre, that even Moriarty, whose sense of cosmic jokes had been sharpened at Shanti Vanum, wanted to discover the Creative Joker and somehow swipe him back. Earl's death, Tess confided, would come from male breast cancer. *Ad Majoram Dei Gloriam.* Or, *Sic Semper Gloria Homines.* Or, trying to avoid Earl's barely delineated male breast as the stricken man bent his shoulder forward, how Moriarty sometimes thought about it: if this be our God, O Israel, fuck Him. Moriarty watched his own hand twist like a goose's neck, and felt a kind of peace born of controlling at least one thing. He prayed a small prayer for Earl's passing without agony and without embarrassment.   One thing about the Jokester: everybody eventually got His point. All one could ask was a decent release from the relentless comedy.

"Thomas, you seem more relaxed today."

The voice drove Moriarty's head into a violent swivel. Father Jerry stood by him, tricked out this day in a long black seminarian's robe, oh, Moriarty remembered those, and some kind of Nepalese hat, pointed like a pyramid and embroidered in red, black, green and yellow Buddhist symbols. The Enlightened One's eye glared prominently from the fabric

"Yes, no longer tight as a power line," Moriarty said.

"This evening we disband," Father Jerry said, sliding into the exercises.

Moriarty followed his regimen to its finish. He waved to his fellows before walking to his cabin where he again looked out at the retreaters until they ended their Tai Chi and went their ways, radiating like spokes from a hub. Moriarty turned to his books. He had two left unread. One was *The City of God.* He picked up *The Canterbury Tales*, thinking he might be ready for another journey.

In the central room of the HQ building, the air sat heavy as fog. Earl sat by the fire picking at the left strap of his overalls. Jim, at the bow window, stared into the middle distance. Harriet-

Julia-Natasha and the nun, Sister Louise who'd been Brother
Louis before her operation, whispered to one another on the love
seat. Tess, frozen-faced, stared into the cold fireplace. Moriarty
sat driven by Chaucer, thinking over, under, around and through
his own life's tale. As usual, it seemed to have no Canterbury
road, no theme, no spine to it, as all good fiction had. Yes, it had
characters, God knew, and settings up the gazoo, and tensions so
many and so thick that they had brought him to Shanti Vanum.
And his life had traveled through ruptures and raptures and, at
times, into that quiddity of human life, un-understanding. He'd
also felt other phenomena of human life that his fellows might
either reject or not recognize. Geese honking under a full moon.
Spring grass just mown. The sweet sliminess of the cauled
newborn. Tracing another's hand with one's heart finger. The
soul's swell at another's achievement. The innocent, unfeigned
act or word or deed. The tracery of cells, nerve endings, planetary
structures that was the body, at times so like a constellation
careening joyously in a star-stricken universe, at times so prey to
cosmic illnesses, the petty and grand treacheries, the cowardices,
the manifold other-blindnesses and the colossal collision of evil
with the frail, too freighted soul. Either way, in the end, a death,
one saying yea, the other nay. Good joke. Bad joke.

Moriarty looked around. Around him what was there except
the evidence that the Creator was autistic, a Maker given to
daydreaming, hallucinations and violent behavior? And if so,
what then?

With Moriarty in mid-question, the door slammed open.
While his fellows whooped, Moriarty stared, struck dumb.
Careening toward them was a composite holiday figure. Ears
of Easter Bunny. Beard of Santa Claus. Large red Valentine's
Day heart on its black velvet breast. Leek in its mouth for St.
David's Day. Burning ember in a paw for St. John's Day. In
the left hand rode St. Nick's pitchfork. The ink-shimmery
bodysuit bore badges, patches, pins, cockades of dozens of
holidays, none of which Moriarty could now identify because

the thing was upon them, whirling without a human sound but with a great clatter of medals and accoutrements and, of course, the bells on the upturned jester's shoes. Father Jerry's blue eyes blazed through the black domino mask. He fetched up with an unbecoming pirouette in the center of his astounded retreaters, then yelped, "Your revels now are ended. Take your souls and go, you fools." But before any of them could move, the priest shook as if electrocuted, pitching forward to sprawl prone before them. One shoe-bell tinkled in the sudden silence. Moriarty noticed in his own paralysis that not a pilgrim moved until Earl bolted to the fallen figure, fingered a pulse and cried, "He's OK. Another fit. Help me, Jim."

Moriarty, heaving deep breaths, watched the burly breast-cancer sufferer and the AIDS boy, assisted by Sister Louise and Harriet-Julia-Natasha, lift Father Jerry as if he were a plank and carry him through the swinging doors toward the priest's chamber.

Tess's voice kept him from answering himself. "Grand mal," Moriarty heard. "He's an epileptic. Damaged goods."

Moriarty pried his eyes from the still-swinging doors. The silence hung like vapor around him and Tess whose mouth, he saw, twitched from the effort of the last words.

"What a God, eh?" she spat at the doors.

"All Soul's Eve?" Moriarty heard himself say. "What a place, eh?"

"Yours or mine?" she asked

"What?" Moriarty said.

"Figure it out. I've got to go help."

"But..."

"My place," the girl said. "My hell. Yours is somewhere else."

"Do I need a handbasket?" Moriarty asked.

Tess smiled as she might at a clumsy child.

"You don't get it, do you?" she said. "You've got your way. Just keep your head up. You're a watcher."

Then she was gone to the "damaged goods," a term that arrow-like struck Moriarty as oxymoronic. He watched the doors flip behind her, then realized he, too, was flipping, but through his image file. He saw the old lady and her dog. He glimpsed the bantam rooster man and the German environmentalist. The large black man. The fugitive white one. The student lady and the divorcee. The happy tormented homosexuals. His three significant other women and his kids. Then Tess and her no-good, brain-blasted husband. All the rest of the Shanti Vanum folk. He wondered if Merton could have made sense of it, or if Merton had ever touched anyone in the way he'd touched the electric cord, all the way to something final. If he, Thomas Moriarty, given his paws, ever would.

Outdoors in the chill dusk Moriarty paused to take a deep breath. Maybe in time he'd know, when he found his cave. Moriarty shivered against the developing night. How long would it take him to hitchhike back to the city? Tess was right. For a while his way may still be the road, although he was pretty sure that another monk's cell or another woman, or even Africa wasn't on the itinerary just yet, not just yet. Moriarty moved down the gravel road toward the highway, thinking about his meditation, and suddenly thought he knew what the Joker smiled about.

III

Who Taught Me To Swim,
Or The Day The Houses
Were Sold

I

My mother taught me to swim. She was a champion swimmer, tutored by Gertrude Ederle, the first female human to swim the English Channel. I'm sure, however, that many female fishes and other seafaring mammals frequently crossed between England and France, bearing eggs and God knows what else. So? What I'm trying to remember is a YMCA not far south of our Chicago home. My mother held my belly as I flailed in the water.

"Jimmy, just move your arms and legs, don't be afraid," I remember.

I knew I had arms and legs, and later in life I learned what they were for. But now I'm in that pool, both of us cold and laced with chemicals, and I'm moving my arms and legs as fast as I can.

Significance? All my adult life I've been swimming, moving as fast as I can against an implacable force. Haven't you? Anyway, I learned to swim in the real sense finally. I learned lots of things at my mother's hand. Not being afraid wasn't one of them.

Fear was my modus vivendi. I don't know why, except my mother and, to the extent he was there, my father instilled dread as if by osmosis. Normal fears I could fathom. I probably wouldn't get polio in the swimming pool, although that was possible, but then again polio victims sometimes recovered by doing exercises in the pool. Same with crossing streets or hitching rides on my sled behind cars when the streets were snow covered or doing wheelies on my clumsy big-tire bike. Those were all known hazards. But there was this other kind of dread that you slept with and a clammy sort of worry that came from the feeling that you might do something wrong, or worse, cause somebody else to do something wrong that would hurt that somebody.

This dread, this pervasive feeling that I was about to do something wrong, led to many minor fears. That I wouldn't do the lettering right in Mrs. Wright's art class, or write 1067 in history about the Norman Conquest, or recognize the Latin ablative absolute in that dead-language class or the proper German verb conjugations. As you can tell, I went to fancy prep places. I thought I was being prepped for college, but other things came along. I digress from fear. But before a dread story, let me tell you about my purest moment: I was on my bike delivering groceries (my father was a believer in the Ben Franklin school of upward mobility) and I stopped on the way back to Petty's delicatessen at the ball field where my friends were playing a pick-up game.

"Hey, grocery kid," Bob Frooman yelled. "Come hit. We need an out." I couldn't refuse. Frooman was a hero in my class. Smart, tough, a Jewish guy headed for the stratosphere.

"Give me a bat."

The pitcher was a skinny kid from the neighboring public school. I'd seen him throw stickball and what we called in

Chicago, "fast pitching." He'd grip the ball across the seams and throw submarine style, like Ewell Blackwell or Dan Quisenberry if you read baseball history. Anyway, I knew the ball would break down and away (later in life my father-in-law told me that was the only way to get Babe Ruth out), so I set up close to the plate, shifted my delivery slips to my left back pocket, and waited. The first two pitches were outside, my friend Kenneth Knutson, the volunteer umpire, said. The base runners on first and second jumped and waved their arms as if that would settle things. The third pitch I remember was a fear-free slider, low but over the outer edge of the plate. I swung, and as if in a dream, the white ball arched toward the green gap in right-center and settled into the rocky outfield between two running kids. I wound up on third. Frooman couldn't believe it.

"You've never hit like that," he said.

I think I said, "You've not watched me enough. Now I have to deliver some strawberry tarts. "

"See you," Frooman said.

Dread didn't disappear with that, sorry to say. Not long after that beautiful smudged ball hit the stony turf, I found myself sitting in the 444 Bar next to Mr. Petty's delicatessen, with my mother. It was a winter evening, the wind blowing hard off Michigan. My delivering was done and I was full of Mrs. Petty's pastries. My father would be struggling home from the stockyards via the El, and Mom was drinking vodka listening to Frank Sinatra on the Wurlitzer. She'd long ago given up her swimming so she baked and cooked and drank to forget that, I now figure, she was married to a man a dozen years older who had ulcers and didn't much like anything except bowling and reading mystery novels.

I remember on one of these occasions asking, "What's wrong, Mom?"

"You'll never know," she said.

This evening, though, I had a clue. A guy in the 444, there every time I got hauled along as Mom's protective company, was habitually amorous toward my mother, who still had a swimmer's body. She'd allow him to sit on the other side of her and chat, but she kept me close, like insulation. Not incidentally, I fulfilled that function in my marriages, too. Anyway, this wintry night he acted drunken cozy. Bill, I think his name was. Every time Sinatra slid up to a high note, Bill would try to put his arm around Mom. The bartender, Jerry, cast eyes at my mother and shook his head. I liked Jerry. He had his lunch sandwiches made at Petty's, and he always acted nice with me.

"Bill," Jerry said. "I don't think Mrs. Anderson wants your attention."

"We'll see," I recall Bill saying. Mom just smiled. I learned later what women meant when they did that: they didn't want the guy but they liked the attention. Jerry eyed Bill all the time he sat by Mom. I wandered the place, studying the pool table, the shuffleboard, wondering about what I later discovered were numbers tickets littering the floor. I looked at the neon flashing on the Wurlitzer. How did they do that? I heard my mother laugh, Bill joining her. I turned away from the jukebox just as the laughter stopped. No one could mistake my father busting into the place. Big. Brawny. Angry. We watched, eyes wide open, when he pulled Bill from the swiveling red-leatherette stool by the collar of his Arrow shirt, shook him like our cat did a mouse, and tossed him into the Wurlitzer. Fortunately, I'd moved aside. I admired the flickering when Bill's head hit the neon like kielbasa. Then he slid to the floor. Dad pulled Mom off her bar stool—she was still holding her glass—and in a calm, Midwestern voice said, "Jimmy, it's time to go." I believe Jerry grinned as Dad muscled us out of the 444. Today, he'd have been worried about liability. That day he admired the honorable gesture. So did I. I had a quick supper of chili and corn souffle. My father, still tense, escorted me to my back bedroom. I heard my mother crying over the sound of the Bears game. I did what I always did. Felt myself to make sure I was there, and opened a sea novel. Mom sneaked to the 444 many times after that. So far as I knew, Bill never went there again, nor did my father. I did know the Wurlitzer was fixed. I could hear it when I passed on my delivery bike.

II

When my last wife hit me with a frying pan—or skillet if you're Southern-born—I remembered in the pain and shame and kielbasa echo a last 444 story. My wife and I were arguing about my behavior, which was terrible I now admit, and I said, "you're a lying whore," which I should have said to myself, since the matters of dispute were whether I'd had too many women and drinks or not. I had, and she was right to be angry and censorious although I think all she said before the blow was "you low-life, stinking son of a bitch." Oddly, in the shock of the frying pan, I revisited the time when my mother (who was the bitch just mentioned) was fresh from a furtive trip to the 444, and I fresh from a frozen-prairie hockey game. We arrived simultaneously to our apartment to find my father, a demon reader, scanning the *Tribune*.

"You're early," my mother said, hurrying off to the bathroom to wash up.

"Good game, Jimmy?"

"Cold," I said.

He nodded, my mom returned, and then my father threw down the paper and said, "I can smell him on you."

My mom fled to my bedroom with me close behind.

My father followed at a slower gait, his heels thumping the hardwood. He pushed open the door with clenched fists.

"You perfidious, fucking bitch," he said. "Just because you're a doctor's daughter and raised in the pink, you think you can do anything."

I didn't know what that meant then. My father's father was a doctor, too. I now know that what he said in rage and hurt was that someone had taken advantage of him in the worst possible way, which is what my skillet-wielding wife also thought.

"Leave us alone," my mother shouted. "All you do is spy and suspect and sit in your chair reading and complaining about your belly while I cook and take care of Jimmy and you have the guts to upbraid me about a drink around the corner."

At that, my father lunged at my mother and slapped her hard across her left cheek. I cried and hid my head in a pillow. My mother picked up my ivory-base reading lamp and hit my father on the head with it. He bled and let out a cry more of anguish than pain. My mother fetched a washcloth to staunch the bleeding. "I'm sorry, sorry," she kept saying, "but I didn't do anything." My father hugged her then. They hugged and went to the bathroom to stop the bleeding and then to their bedroom, where I'd once found Trojans in my father's dresser.

"Jimmy, don't worry," my mother said as she shut my door. I wiped my face and picked up *The Red Badge of Courage*, reading until I was sleepy.

Reading always helped me. After my wife slugged me and told me to get the fuck out and I saw no great skull damage was done, I took *Middlemarch* with me to the motel. In the morning I called my lawyer, who was used to this. He said, "OK, once again into the breach. You really need another hobby. Wife-collecting, boozing and floozie hunting is making you poor and sick. Do you ever think of the trajectory of your life?"

Obviously, my old friend Bob Frooman was a thoughty kind of barrister. "Trajectory, eh?" I'd been an artillery officer once, and trajectory supposedly meant the three-dimensional path, often an arc, of a moving body, but with guns it also meant time fired to time detonated. That made more sense in this frying pan situation. So did Frooman's analysis of my past and current way of life. What had made me the way I was? I couldn't blame the parents. They were both dead. School had been easy, and so were the swim teams up through college. Karma might be the culprit, but so far I'd been pretty lucky in the things of this world, except for the three wives. You can't sneeze at a thriving real-estate development business, or the increasingly noble houses I bought for my households. True, I'd had no children to ruin or otherwise, and that might be bad in karma scoring, but then neither had Jesus, so far as we know and while he'd had that unpleasantness on the cross, he was supposedly divine, which isn't a bad outcome.

Frooman had an opinion. He expressed it while drawing up the divorce papers.

"These had better be the last," he said. "You've still got big assets, but giving them to wives doesn't increase them, and the development market's getting soft. But that's economics. The main thing you need to do is to get the hell out of Chicago. Stop driving yourself and those around you crazy, including me. Maybe you could just fall in love and suffer in normal ways. Here, sign these."

III

We swim every day in the sea. The sun, seldom absent, burnishes her long dark hair. Our house isn't grand, but selling all the other houses and stuff just before the market surface-dived, means neither of us needs to work except at what we like. My former wives are happy with their portions. All have remarried, one to a defrocked minister, another to a low-ratings TV anchorman, and the last to an advance man for the Illinois Republican Committee. All three shiver in the wind off Lake Michigan except when they're not on a get-the-fuck-away-from-this trip to Santa Fe or St. Thomas or the occasional taxpayer-paid junket. We exchange cordial e-mails on holidays.

Isabel, that's her name, and I also travel, sometimes to ski in the Alps or sail the Med or sightsee someplace that seems interesting. But we travel more often to Africa or the Philippines to inspect the aid work of our little foundation, cutely named

Swim or Sink. Isabel, who's Spanish, still doesn't get the name, but it's my money so I got to choose. I met her in Madrid, on a post-divorce trip my lawyer Bob Frooman ordered me to take. She taught at the Instituto Ingles where I was taking Spanish lessons. Now my Spanish is pretty fair. There's nothing like sleeping with a foreigner to learn a language. Luckily her English is nearly perfect, as I found out on our first formal date, long before we slept together, when she said, "You're nice. You're rich. But you're injured and angry and, how do we say?, selfish, *egoísta*. You need to get away from you, *comprende?*" In short order I found it as true as she is. We haven't married, although with my record, it's not impossible. If we do, Isabel wants to adopt a child from one of the countries Sink or Swim works in. She almost kidnapped an Eritrean kid on our last trip, but I told her to wait. I think she'd be a great mother. She does a good job with me. I hate to admit it, but I love her, even when she's mad at a bad verb I employ, or when I insist on going with her to the a big-box *hipermercado*—oh, how many of those, too, I developed—to buy this or that necessity for our villa. It's near Malaga and it's on the beach. Isabel's a great help in our trips back to the USA to put the arm on donors, and to follow them up with letter, e-mails, phone calls and invoices. In the Spanish-speaking nations she's a terrific fund-raiser. She's charming and easy on the eyes. She's persistent in the appeals for money or food or diapers or water or milk or medicine.

She's also cunning, not above using gossip or mild threats ("what will your spouse/lover/banker/maid/mother/aunt/god-mother/father/godfather/uncle/best friend/governmental colleagues think?") She also has a temper, as I've learned, but she doesn't strike anyone except verbally, as in "don't shout at me, or I'll leave." These times she sulks and is cold in bed. Her business nickname is *La Bruja Buena*, the Good Witch, often said by those she importunes with a shrug. I call her my *brujula*, which means compass.

That's not to say everything is wonderful. I still remember my childhood. In a way I'm still delivering groceries. I still remember the terror of my mother and father's marriage, and the screaming nonsense and wounds. I also remember many good times in my life. Being loved despite it all, lovemaking, good books, sports, especially *beisbol* although soccer's gaining, and good meals and wine (God, I love a good Rioja off a zinc bar in Pamplona when the bulls are running), snow and sun, sea and land, many opposites, but not good and bad. These days I opt only for good, even when it's bad, as it is with the fly-bitten children and hungry men and women and kids with guns, all the real terror of war, of raids and burning homes, of rape and pillage and general inhumanity, and of famine and pestilences. I have malaria now, which isn't pleasant, but I have good doctors and medicine, which is more than the thousands have who die of that and worms and AIDS and a hundred other horrors. Fortunately, Isabel seems immune to disease. She's abnormally healthy. She holds me when I shake.

Can I say I'm happy? On a day like this, when the sun is high but the sand is cool, and a gentle breeze is coming off the Sahara, and we're full of a nice white wine and Basque-style fish, I'm beyond happy, whatever may be over the horizon. When the sun gets too hot, we head for the sea. Isabel's not a good swimmer yet, so for a couple of reasons I always manage at some point to put my hands under her stomach, and tell her, "Love, just move your arms and legs. Don't be afraid. I'm holding you." Then we both laugh and splash each other.

MEN LUST, WOMEN CONCEIVE, NOTHING MATTERS

My best friend uttered that on his deathbed. I would have taken it as a sour comment on the human condition had he been anyone but "Don Blanco," a nickname given him by the Catalans among whom we lived. He was white in ways and was human. But he belonged to the sorry sort who find little to like about being human, except their humanity. His real name was Joseph (a.k.a. Giuseppe) Negro, so named because his parents when they came to the United States couldn't understand what the immigration officer was asking them, so when they were asked to pick the white or black boxes on the form, they chose black, which was their preferred color, the one of mourning. Joe was a friend, as I've said. His story matters because it rings much with mine. When he was dying and said these words, I took his hand, his spindly right hand, and said, "Rest, I'll take care of it." Not long after, he died.

I should make clear that I am male, and so was Joe. Our friendship went back to the Last Great War, meaning when the enemies were known as "Krauts" and "Japs." Before we found out that what America truly stood for wasn't democracy so much as saving markets. I remembered that when he gave my index finger a feeble squeeze before passing away. I thought, hell, it's better than shrapnel. Joe and I shared more than memories. We shared many women, including two wives and this town we lived in, a village on the northwest coast of Mallorca, which is itself an outpost of Spain, but nicely located, just south of France, as Joe used to say, and a bit north of Paradise.

A bit north puts it well. Our town hugged the northwestern coast mountains, closer to France than Africa. The stone houses lay strewn about the hills like dice. Mine was the closest to the rocky beach. Joe's was on the main street, such as it was. That was our difference, I suppose, like when George Gershwin told Oscar Levant to take the top bunk on an L.A.-bound train because "that's the difference between genius and talent."

But I digress. Flash backward to 1969, on the cusp of the real world, and understand that the demise of the Great Poet wasn't planned. Joe at first intended only to deflate him with a prank, one of those things we did at seventeen when we weren't scraping out a foxhole, like firing flares at night so we could read Bill Mauldin's cartoons in *Stars and Strips*. Hell, the Germans knew where we were anyway and Willy and Joe made us feel as if we'd survive the war. We did, and on the GI bill we stayed in Europe, took some courses at the Sorbonne, drank a lot, chased women, and when we arrived on the resort island, decided to stay. Some still think we just freeloaded, but that's only envy talking. We invested unearned family income and Army pay, using the *Herald-Tribune*'s business news as a guide. That worked. We worked at odd jobs, construction mostly, and learned Catalan and Spanish. Joe already knew Italian, and I could translate from mainland Spanish so we did well in the word game. Our first wife was Danish, and she was sweet as a pastry. Name of Meridith, because her father was English. Joe married her first, and I got her second after he went off to Bali for some years.

She died three years ago, safe at home in Denmark. But again, I digress. The Great Poet's death is the topic.

It's 1969: Bobby and Martin are dead. Tricky Dick is littering the White House. Kissinger is acting like Bismarck. I'm still smarting from Joe's purloining of our second wife, a sweet woman from Naples. I think he got her with native pillow talk. I couldn't do that. Too brooding, my best female companion said of me before she defected to Philadelphia in search of more social security than I could provide. Anyway, Joe decided that the Great Poet was too full of himself, too preening, too much in control of our village, issuing forth from his H-shaped house to delight the populace, captivate foreign and domestic women, and generally rule the roost. I knew him well, had written about him, and so was Joe's chosen accomplice. As they say now, I had issues with the poet. Not moral issues—that was Joe's domain. Mine were mortal. So I agreed. We would insert a fatal worm into him out of some piques and flaws of character, ours and/or his.

It started in earnest one autumn day when the mist was hanging around the surrounding mountains, when Joe, drunk, said to me, also drunk, "I know, let's kill him with kindness."

Now, Joe and the Great Poet had long differed. The poet was a WWI hero. Joe was a staff sergeant Milo Minderbinder out of WWII. I'd been a lowly noncom in a transportation outfit, which is how I met Joe, when he falsified papers to get a couple of back-echelon, deuce-and-a-halfs to go into Reims and loot champagne, caviar, truffles, cigarettes and a couple of working girls to pass around his supply unit to which I'd been attached. There festered in Joe a number of public humiliations by the Great Poet, as when he pilfered one of Joe's girls simply by saying in rhyme that she was a Goddess, a benevolent *duende* possessed of such power that he could only buy her houses, commit polite cunnilingus, and write songs for her. Joe had unsuccessfully wooed her with strong spirits and a penis that I can testify from war brothels didn't lack its own power. But the poet had money, fame, and two powerful family webs in England. Joe and I had war benefits and that money our families had left us. I could live on mine, plus I worked. I published travel articles, fabricated feature pieces, got a few stories and odd things in print and flogged them shamelessly in lectures.   Joe worked angles, like importing Asian furniture, particularly from Bali, and selling phony impressionist paintings to the culturally ignorant folks he met and charmed on his frequent journeys.

But let me return to the plot to kill the Great Poet with kindness. Even I, who had great regard for nothing of Joe's except his Medici good looks and his cat-quick instincts, had to marvel.

"With kindness," he repeated. "Lust, conception and indifference." He coughed then, sending a plume of phlegm into the chilled air surrounding what we called the "upper bar," which meant it was on the main village road and ran tabs. Behind my Fundador I nursed my single grudge: the man had stolen three books from me, not the bound kind, the ideas kind.

"Let's lure him with an exorcism," I said. The Great Poet loved exorcisms, had often written about them. I did, too, although I hadn't been successful in exorcising my ghosts. Once I told the poet my deepest secret, that I had ordered two plump SS Germans out of my jeep somewhere near Reims—I was transporting them for Military Intelligence, one of the great oxymoronic phrases of any war. I shot them in the gut with the Thompson M1A1 I carried, took the ropes off, and left them there to be counted as victims of pissed-off French Resistance leftovers. They fell like sacks, just like in the movies, saying only "nein, nein, bitte." Joe laughed about that.   His main contribution to the war's atrocities consisted of screwing a German corporal up the butt, then giving him a pack of cigarettes, as I recounted to the Great Poet who sighed, fondled his wattles, and told me that these were nothing compared to the Western Front, the Battle of the Somme, when with his Webley he shot five Germans and one cowardly Welshman from his regiment, and that was just in one day. He admitted he'd drunk a bottle of brandy beforehand. He reminded me that an American general once said war was hell. He said he did more prisoners later, in addition to his duties as an infantry officer, before he was wounded and spent the remainder of the Great War in an asylum for the shell-shocked. I fell silent. In our many meetings afterwards the subject never came up, and I knew neither of us had ever committed civil murder. In fact, once the nightmares passed, we agreed, the Great Poet and I, that killing any living thing except with kindness was inhumane. But driving out devils seemed within bounds.

"Exorcisms," Joe had exclaimed. "Fuck me, if that isn't terrific."

We agreed, then, that our mutual humiliation of the Great Poet must involve a woman. Not just a woman, and not an obvious woman like his current wife, and not one of our former women (who wouldn't speak to us anyway) but an *extranjera* Woman-Woman. Our problem was that neither of us knew such a creature, nor could attract one. What to do? Well, as believers say—and the Great Poet was one—Kismet will provide. Really, I hope not, and I did those several years ago. I'd just as soon not be judged on my life, but rather my life's fictions, just like the poet. But in this case, Mr. or Mrs. Kismet came through. My summons came when Miguel the firewood man knocked on my door to tell me that I owed him for the load of wood he'd just dumped on my doorstep and that Don Blanco was in the upper bar and wanted to see me. I handed him the money and trudged up. Joe's emphysema had even by then progressed to the point where he worried me and some old soldier's honor forced me up the hill. I found him at our usual round table on the terrace—it was a bright spring morning with wisps of clouds teasing the mountains that cupped our village. Across from his coffee sat a leggy blonde.

"This is Kristin," Joe said. "She speaks English, French, German and Icelandic. That's where she's from. She's interested in the poet's notions about Goddesses."

"I think men must believe that Goddesses are," Kristin said.

I ordered a *caratillo* with extra brandy. Kristin appeared ready for anything. I wondered if this should be the time I said, "set 'em up Joe, we're drinking, my friend, to the end of a sweet episode," but I said nothing except hello and asked my friend what he had in mind. In retrospect, it involved devils of various makings. We sat there, the three of us, while Joe chatted up Kristin, and then as if by cue, the Great Poet appeared at the bend of the road, heading our way for his coffee after stopping at the *tienda* for his mail, wearing his formidable, broad-brimmed black hat and his operatic cloak. We watched him advance until he ascended to the terrace. Like an iron filing to a magnet, he drew himself to Kristin, ignoring Joe, whom he detested, and flicking a nod at me, said in something that must have been some Nordic tongue a phrase that made her smile. He then retreated to English.

"You've met my good friend, Don Blanco" the poet said. "The nonentity to my right is Gerald Fitzpatrick. If he'd had the wit, he'd have forged the Howard Hughes biography." This, known to everyone then, referred to another writer of the neighboring island of Ibiza, who had concocted a Hughes bio on the false notion that since Howard was infamously nuts and reclusive, no one would ever know.   I did not remind him that he had appropriated my ideas for an American Revolutionary War novel, a history of pari-mutuel gambling, and a work on the origin of Goddess icons.

"Thanks, " I said.

"I'm possessed," Kristin said. Joe smiled.

"And I'm an alert drunk," Joe said, pointing to his coffee.

"I'm possessed," Kristin repeated, turning on a searchlight smile. It was if the Great Poet and Kristin had disappeared into the mountain mists. Joe and I were absent. That's when Joe said, "We got him now. Nothing is forgiven, least of all lust."

I must digress again. Joe's death throe is in full momentum. He wants to tell me something, as most dying people do. My father said, "watch carefully, I won't be doing this again." But Joe's nearly last message was different.

"You remember when the poet said he'd cleanse Kristin."

"Yes," I said, I'd have said anything to spare him the pain of speech.

"You remember we went to your house for the ceremony?"

"Yes."

Joe's face had that death-mask look now, the features tightened and white, as though he were being summoned.

"I lied when I told him, after, that I'd screwed her and he went nuts and started his swimming thing. I never screwed her. Listen, too, I did see something come out of her at the exorcism, like steam. Don't tell him, please."

Then Joe was dead, empty as a birthday party balloon. I never did tell him that I also had seen the something come out of Kristin that day that smelled like pot, and that I had screwed her later and myself and the Great Poet in more ways than any of us knew.

Before my place was warm from the Swedish wood stove, the poet told Kristin to strip, not something she was unused to. Joe and I took seats next to the fireplace, which also lent heat to the white-washed room. The colloquy began.

"Where does a Goddess go bad?" the poet asked. Joe whispered, "in the XX chromosome thing." I didn't care. She was gorgeous, toked to the gills, and seemed then as dumb as a wheelbarrow of clams. Everything I wanted in a Goddess.

That, however, wasn't what the poet was interested in. In my little *entrada* there had to be candles, many candles. And wine, much wine. The poet took photos of the stoned Goddess on the daybed. And, of course, he recited poetry, lots of poetry. One the poet was especially fond of. I can only remember the first line: "She tells her love while half asleep..." That was true. Half-asleep was she, and so were Joe and I. The exorcism itself, in retrospect, came like a premature ejaculation. The poet circled the girl, who was babbling in that odd Nordic tongue probably related in some esoteric way to Basque. He chanted in Latin (I had four years and Joe was Italian so we parsed that), what we figured was Greek, then some tongue we couldn't identify. He waved his big black hat, fondled her a bit, and finally in good British English, shouted "Devil, you have lusted and conceived yourself in her. Get thee hence." The strange steam plume started, I thought. The poet turned and pointed at us. Joe and I started for the door. But Kristin beat us to it. In seductively good English, she said, "You're all fucked up." She pulled on clothes. The big wood doors closed on her. The poet smiled before saying, "The feminine endings are usually a soft vowel." We drank to that, and many things.

When dawn peered over the mountains, the three of us weaved down the rocky path to the sea. The poet peeled off to his underwear, and picked his way to a large rock below the headland. Joe and I sat in the shuttered beachfront cafe, pulling on a bottle of wine I'd providentially brought along. The poet, even at 73, possessed a good lean body. When he reached his favorite rock, he threw himself into the sea. He swam with steady strokes toward us, pulled up, saluted, and strode back up the path toward the mouth of the *torrente* that flowed into the sea. He picked up his clothes, putting them in the crook of his left arm. He waved town-ward. We turned to see Kristin at the top of the rock steps leading down to the coast, clad in translucent white.

How she got there we could later only surmise. A second thought about the poet's exorcism? A final kick of the Marrakesh Express? Whatever, she was there and she and the poet, right hand in hers and his hat on, ascended the path, to go through the silver-leafed olive trees and the lowing sheep to the H-shaped house. She stayed with him, although living for appearance's sake in a house next to his, constructed by him for her. We all became, as the poet put it, "lovers-in-law." She closed his eyes and put penny-pieces on them when he died thirteen years later. He did his best work during that time. She had two children, a boy and a girl. The progenitor was unknown. The boy was stillborn. The girl hit her head diving from the poet's rock and drowned when she was five. The day the poet's spirit departed she left her house and us, without a word.

After it all, at the memorial service to which I took Joe, himself about ready to be put feet first into the village graveyard, we exchanged guarded glances with the village priest. The priest shook his head at us, but after the words had been said, when we gathered for the celebration at the dead poet's house, the priest told Joe and me that we'd done the poet a kindness. "The devil works in mysterious ways," he said, in halting English. "When you think to cast him out, sometimes he takes the hint, sometimes not." The day was cold, and I saw a plume rise from the priest's lips as we stood in line to commiserate with the poet's last forbearing widow and the surviving six children from his marriages. I wanted to ask the priest if adultery and stealing books and ideas and killing Germans could be so dismissed. He turned away. I asked Joe.

"Don't believe any of the crap," he gasped. "Theft is natural. Look at politics. And killing is killing, sometimes good, sometimes bad. Let's hit the wine"

We did, and I did again at Joe's service. Kristin didn't come back from Iceland for that. Only three people attended. Me, Joe, and the priest, granted leave from an old-priest's home in the province's capital city. When the priest was finished sending Joe off, I asked him again if kindness could kill, if something headed bad could wind up good.

"My poor son," he said. "It takes a lot of *suerte*." Luck was everything? Nice, but an old idea, I thought, and I wanted to ask him if we all were just animals, made for lust and making babies and creating empty ceremonies, as we do with literature, creating them to celebrate such mysteries. I wanted to ask him if that was the rule the Romans operated under all those centuries ago. But his driver took him by the arm. He waved weakly at me before getting in the old black Fiat. I stood for a bit on the hillside, savoring the lemon-scented, on-shore breeze, before trudging downhill to my house, where I would have a coffee, a large cognac, utter a short secular prayer, a toast to Joe and the poet and Kristin and luck and kindness. Then I'd wait.

House Call

Rosebud Reservation, South Dakota: 1912

B etween the babies crying and the groans of the smelly old squaws, Edna West Henderson was just about to go berserk. Bad enough that she was stuck in this ancient, cold house, with snow piled all around, and a leaky wood stove to stoke and coal oil lamps to fill, linens to wash and instruments to boil and their meals to fix. Worse, she'd missed two periods, and she was regular as a school clock, so there was little doubt she was pregnant, even if she didn't feel too nauseous or, for that matter, different at all. Except bored and tired. Days like this she wished she was back in the parsonage with her foster parents, even if they were strict. But then, naturally, she wouldn't be married to Jerry, and that did make up for some things. She guessed she'd tell him tonight. He never noticed physical things about her, hardly, which was odd since as a doctor he noticed just about everything about these darned Indians.

Edna checked her boiling pot. Jerry's instruments lay in the bubbling water. The heat and vapor had frosted the windows so that she couldn't see out. Didn't matter. Nothing but snow and the few other houses of this wonderful town of White River.

Edna picked up her copy of *McClure's* and dreamed again. One day, she vowed, she'd live in a grand house as these ladies did, and serve tea, and wear gowns and give fancy parties at home and at the country club, and have shiny, expensive automobiles instead of the old flivver that the Indian agent had lent Jerry, that and his old team of horses good only for glue and to get up the trails into where the Lakota Sioux lived in those horrid clapboard government houses or their smoky tipis they traveled with. Might as well be gypsies. Edna just knew she was born for better than what she had now, but she reminded herself, looking at the lovely long dresses sketched in the magazine, that she was only nineteen and there were better things to come.

Even better, she supposed, to be here doctoring the Indians than have Jerry fighting them in the old days, or over there with those horrible Turks and Greeks and people. But, maybe not. For a moment she pictured herself getting the telegram, and weeping over her heroic dead husband, killed while doing valiant duty in a field hospital, and she could see herself beautiful in black at the funeral with all the soldiers shooting into the air, and the flag, and the white granite cross with Jerry's name on it. And didn't war widows get some money, too? But Jerry's eyesight wasn't good enough for the Medical Corps, whatever eyes had to do with it. So they were here. Besides, if she were pregnant, that would ruin the whole pretty picture.

"Edna? Edna, are they ready? I need them." Jerry's voice wrenched Edna back to White River. She dropped *McClure's* on the kitchen table, carefully picked up the pot and poured the water into the sink. Carrying the pot with a towel, she walked to the front parlor where Jerry had established his treatment room. She stepped on tiptoes past the Indians hunched in the hall against the wall. The smell of grease and sweat and whiskey wrinkled her nose. She shouldered back the half-open parlor door.

"Here, darling," Edna said.

Jerome Henderson looked up from his patient, to be struck again by his young wife's beauty. She positively glowed, from her swept-up auburn hair to her tiny feet, and all between pleased him, not least the curves of bosom and hips. In this forsaken place, amongst these poor, ailing and alien natives, she shone like a beacon guiding him to happiness. Well, Jerome corrected himself, certainly happiness as much as could be had here. But she put up with all this so well, and it helped both of them knowing it was just a first job, all he could get right out of Creighton Medical School. A house, a practice, an automobile. Not too bad, really. And certainly all he could want in the way of medical experience. These people had every disease known to him, many courtesy of the whites who'd invaded these lands. Progress. Jerome admitted there was medical progress, and industrial and maybe artistic, but look at what went on, what we'd invented. Machine guns. Dreadnoughts. Artillery shells that tore, maimed, killed, like the cavalry had done to those poor devils at Wounded Knee when he was a tyke. Like the folks in the Balkans now, fighting, killing in the name of religion, but really for land, wealth, power. What was it all about? Millions dead around the globe just in the Age of Progress. Progress?

"Wonderful, dear. Put them there, will you?" He watched Edna's graceful move to the instrument case. They'd taught her well at Reverend Gray's. She moved like a lady, knew how to cook and sew and what silverware to use. Rather remarkable, actually.

"How many are out there?" Jerome asked.

"The hall's full, and the front bedroom, too."

"Looks like a thundering day again. But I'll hurry. I promise."

Edna's smile flashed across to him, and then she was out the door headed toward her chores. Poor girl, but nineteen, tending to the household, and feeding the team when he didn't have time, going with him, when he needed her, out into the reservation. Jerome hoped the winter wouldn't be too severe, though it was starting out like a bitch kitty. It was their first, and the agent warned them about getting stuck on the trails. You'll freeze quicker than water, he'd said. Find you in the spring, hard as rock candy. Well, she was sweet enough anyway.

Jerome turned his attention to the patient, a Lakota woman of some middling age. He couldn't tell, and they never said. She had a boil the size of a walnut on the back of her neck, glowing raw red against her coppery skin. Henderson painted the area with tincture of iodine.

"This will hurt. I have to cut. You understand." He moved the side of his hand like a knife.

The woman nodded and bowed her head. Strange, he thought, these people. In the six months here, he'd seen them bear hideous pain with scarcely a murmur. Women in childbirth. Men with knife wounds in their guts. Even dying from the influenza raging everywhere, as so many were despite what he could do, they stayed silent until the death rattle shook them. Then the women started to keen and there was plenty of noise, but before that it was like they had a pact with the Great Spirit to endure life's sufferings with dignity. Whites didn't, at least the ones he'd treated during his internship in Omaha.

Jerome took the newly boiled scalpel and the draining cup. With a quick, deft stroke, he sliced into the infection. The pus spurted, then rolled into the cup, streaked with blood, like a fancy custard. He pressed gently to empty the tissue. Not a sound from the woman. He painted again with the iodine, then dressed the wound. He tapped the woman.

"All done. You keep it clean. Clean. Wash. Do you understand? With soap."

The woman nodded. She stood to go.

"I know," she said. "Soap. Thank you. You bring good medicine." She moved through the door ahead of him.

"Next," said Jerome Henderson. "Next."

They came and went all afternoon. He treated more boils, and scabies, and catarrh brought on by the hot tipis and cold weather. Two men and a woman were back with syphilis, and he gave them the arsphenamine, knowing while it might help, even cure them, they'd soon get it again, just as they couldn't stay out of the whiskey. It made Jerome ill to see the whites come up from Valentine and Cody, and fan out with their rotgut liquor, against the regulations but with the Indian agent's wink, into the tribal communities. Some of it they adulterated with methanol, and then he'd have to treat the victims for the tremors and nerve damage, though he couldn't do much, not when the brain went dead. Now he vaccinated some children against the smallpox and tetanus, and with willow splints he set a broken carpus, result of a horse kick. He dispensed aspirin and terpin hydrate and codeine, and iodine pills against the goiter, and as much advice about cleanliness and sanitation as he could. Dysentery was nearly as big a problem as the flu, and he was getting low on the morphine pills that stopped the flux. But, without cleaning up the water supplies out there on the reservation proper, things'd continue bad. They sure didn't need any typhoid here, too, but he bet that'd be next.

At five, the hall and bedroom sat empty. Jerome rubbed his neck while cleaning up the room. What day was it, anyway? Not that it mattered, except Sundays when the one preacher in town had a nondenominational service. He'd been raised staunch Roman Catholic, and he still believed, mostly, even if practicing a little medicine had convinced Jerome that some doctrines didn't fit reality too snugly. Edna, now, had been raised in that Methodist parsonage, but she said she'd convert if he asked her. Right now, what Jerome wanted to ask her was if there was coffee on the stove.

There was, but Edna wasn't in the kitchen. He found her upstairs, in their bedroom, turning one of his shirt collars.

"They gone?" she asked.

"Yes, poor devils. And that was just the ordinary stuff. I've got to go over to the quarantine now."

"You've got blood on your shirt again," she said. "Can't you wear the apron?"

"I will."

Jerome knew she felt pouty because all either of them seemed to do was work. She was especially touchy about the laundry, since even with the squaw who came to help, Edna had to supervise, and heat the water, and there wasn't any place except the dining room to hang things to dry, not in this weather. Jerome finished his coffee.

"I'll take a quick look at the quarantine, then come right back."

Edna flashed him a nod and a smile before going back to her mending. She heard him clomp down the steps and stop for his overcoat before she heard the front door close. Yes, she'd try to tell him tonight, if he ever got finished with these Indians. She knew what he'd do now. Go into the old rooming house where all the influenza cases were quarantined, and expose himself to the germs. Bend over to touch and take the temperature of them all, and give them the aspirin and make sure Mrs. Jackson, the preacher's wife, was giving them plenty of fluids, and he'd worry himself sick about the ones he knew wouldn't make it. They'd buried three last week, two old men and a six-year-old girl. Not exactly buried, though. Hacked a hole in the ground was more like it, as if planting a seed that would never grow. Still, Jerome was that way, and she loved him, so she'd just have to put up with his life. It was time to fix supper anyway, and after that they could sit and read and talk and go to bed, and then she'd tell him she was in the family way.

Years later, Edna often told the tale of how it didn't happen that way that night. Her civilized friends would utter mock-horrified gasps and oh-my-dear-please titters, although Edna told it out of a fierce grasp of the past and the way they'd been.

They'd hardly finished supper. The remains of the venison steaks, boiled potatoes, and dried corn still sat on the table while the coffeepot bubbled on the kerosene range. Jerome related a success with an influenza patient, while Edna thought about a hot bath with perfumed salts, and then her confession and some sweet lovemaking. Heavens! How she did enjoy that, especially in the down-quilted bed on a cold night, with the stars bright as beads, the windows frosted with their deep breathing, and the snow locked out. At such times, White River didn't seem so bad. Or even now, when Jerome's hand lay on hers, and they fell silent, listening to the winter wind squeak around the house, and the coffeepot sing. Afterward, she'd often asked who heard the other sounds first? The clank of the buckboard and the horses' snorting, then the running, hard footsteps and the frenzied pounding on the door?

No matter. Jerome went. She heard an Indian's guttural staccato sounds, and Jerome replying, "Yes, yes, let me get my things, yes, stay here." Edna felt the chill from the hallway. She rose, for some reason clutching herself around the chest. Jerome appeared in the doorway.

"Darling, sorry, but a woman's got bad birthing trouble. I've got to go. Don't know how long I'll be."

He already wore his heavy coat and boots. He carried his medical bag and his gloves. A scarf wound around his neck, beneath the wide-brimmed felt hat that dwarfed his face.

"I'll come, too. I can help," Edna heard herself say. What on earth possessed her?

Jerome stared, then nodded. She could help, he knew. There'd be people there she could keep away, and in the matter of anatomy and bloody details she'd shown significant intestinal fortitude. He half-suspected she had some Indian in her. Nobody really knew her parentage. Besides, living at the preacher's farm, she'd seen plenty of birthing, albeit among the lower animals.

"All right, hurry. Dress warm. We're in the wagon."

Neither Edna nor Jerome exactly recalled the journey out. The snow wasn't deep, thank God, no more than two inches, and the half-moon cast plenty of light. But the wind cut through even their heavy wool coats and the scarves they tied over their faces, so that their noses and lips numbed. The Indian man sat hunched on the driver's board, urging his ponies into a jolting trot, saying not a thing. He wore a thin buckskin coat and a round, black hat with an eagle feather stuck in the band. In the moonlight, his face looked sculpted of red granite. They pounded south along the main road, then cut off on an eastward trail. Jerome could make out the ruts of the man's trip into town, and thought, this must be serious. Usually their granny-women delivered the babies. He hoped his bag had what he might need.

He looked over at Edna. With one scarf tied down over her winter bonnet and under her chin and the other around her face she looked like a highwayman with a toothache. Frost coated the scarf at her mouth and nose. Her gloved hands were up under her armpits, and she stamped her feet to keep feeling in them. But she hadn't complained at all. Jerome peered ahead for some sign of life. The man hadn't said how far he'd come, but from the look of his ponies, it hadn't been too far. If it'd been a long way east, he'd have fetched the sawbones in Hidden Timber, though that drunken old ex-cavalry doctor wasn't good for much more than psoriasis and the occasional amputation. Jerome caught a whiff of wood smoke. The Indian was driving the ponies southward again, now, on a smaller trail, probably toward the Keya Paha River. He estimated they drove another ten minutes before he saw a light up ahead, and in another five, they were there. He nudged Edna.

"Lucky. He's a cabin Indian."

She mumbled something through the scarf, but he only caught the words "who's lucky," before the Indian was lifting her down, and he was off the buckboard himself, headed toward the cottonwood-log cabin. Just inside the door, he and Edna both recoiled. The one room reeked of sweat and blood and coal oil and wood smoke. A roaring fire in the hearth made it feel like the steam baths at the Omaha YMCA, and Jerome felt his own sweat start. Three old Indian women kneeled by the birth pallet, and around them moved a female shaman sprinkling something from a buffalo horn. In one corner, by the fireplace, hunkered a young man, no doubt an older son, and in the other, three small children and a teenage girl. The Indian who'd fetched them stationed himself like a statue against the closed door. Jerome had a fleeting picture of how it would have been fifty years ago, the laboring woman in the birth tipi attended only by the old wives, and if the birth was difficult, a transverse lie or a breech, the slow death and the corpse up in the trees in the Lakota Sioux way. But these people were half-white in their ways, too often the bad half. Jerome saw that Edna had stripped off her coat, scarves and bonnet.

"Oh, my God, oh, my God," she was saying. "Jerome, Jerome." He looked at the rude pallet and then he was throwing off his things, too, and shouting at the Indian who must be the father, "Get them out. Get them out, all out now, except you and the children. Get them out." He shouted like a madman, and flapped his arms. The sheer sight of it likely galvanized the Indians, this shortish white man in his white-man's suit and little face-hair moustache and eyeglasses, screaming and making herding gestures. The Indian man started to shout, too, and he and Jerome and Edna began pushing people out into the cold. They went, except for the female shaman who waved her buffalo horn and talisman stick and shrieked in Lakota at the father, probably some kind of curse, and braced herself against the doorjamb.

"For Christ's sake, let her stay," Jerome hollered, motioning toward the corner where the son had been. He noticed the teenage girl comforting the young ones and, from the corner of his eye, saw the father drinking from a stoneware mug. He whiffed the pungent rotgut smell. But the overpowering smell now was blood and fear, and for the first time he heard the woman's moans, low and weak, like a bass fiddle string plucked and sustained.

"Edna, some hot water, and find some rags. We've got to clean her up and get that baby out. Edna!"

Jerome saw his wife start, shudder, then rip her eyes away from the laboring Indian woman and hurry to the cookstove. He looked more closely at the squaw. Not a pretty sight. The woman had bled a lot after the sac burst, he saw, onto the blankets folded beneath her, and she could barely keep her squatting position. She rocked, moaning, her face, her braids, slick with sweat. He wondered at her age. If that boy was eighteen, she could be anywhere from thirty to forty-five, depending on when she'd been given away, which depended on her dowry. She wasn't a pretty woman, particularly not now, with a prominent nose and puffy cheeks and a blocky body. Hard to give away. He went to her, squatted and put his hands on her shoulders.

"I'm Dr. Henderson. From White River. Come to help. Please, now, lie down. I can help better if you do. Please now, lie down. We have to get the baby out."

The woman rocked on, her eyes glazed and unfocused. She didn't seem to see him. A contraction seized the woman, but weakly. He heard the moans take on a melody. Her birth song? Death song?

He pushed her back gently and felt the counterforce.

"Please, now. You must lie down. I will help. You must lie down so I can take the baby."

"Doctor, can I help?"

Jerome turned to see the teenage girl. "Is this your mother?"

"Yes."

The girl spoke well. Must be good in the Bureau school. "Please tell her she must lie down so I can help. We don't want her to die, or the baby."

The girl knelt by her mother's side. Jerome heard her whispering in Lakota. A stream of words. The woman's eyes cleared and came up to meet Jerome's. More words. Then the woman nodded and, with the girl's help, collapsed back on the pallet. The girl held her mother's hand, and kept speaking to her.

Jerome spread the woman's legs and saw the trouble. The baby was breech, one foot in the vaginal canal, which meant the baby was twisted. Trouble on trouble, and he was no expert at this. Another contraction came.

"Jerry?"

Edna held a pan of hot water. He opened his bag for the strong naphtha soap, then washed quickly. No gloves. He'd have to feel this. He poured a weak solution of perchloride of mercury over his hands. He reached for the ammonia ampule. Might help her contract. She was too weak.

"Edna?"

She took the ampule and snapped it under the woman's nostrils. The woman coughed, shook, but perked up.

"Do that whenever she seems to flag," he told Edna and, rolling up his shirt sleeves, bent to his work.

Telling the story later, Edna could see it all, even if she couldn't frame the words just right. But she had it all as clear as when it happened, and she'd not since been as proud of Jerry, despite his great things. She saw herself kneeling at the woman's head, across from the girl. Saw herself with the ampules and, when Jerry told her, with the bite stick for the woman's mouth, when Jerry took the scalpel and cut down the vagina to widen the opening. "Major episiotomy," he said. The woman's teeth crunched on the stick and a low sound escaped her, but nothing more. Edna remembered the woman's husband turning away in his corner to drink the whiskey.

"Edna, if the pain gets too bad and she starts to thrash, you hold this over her nose, and put just a few drops on it. Not much. I want her awake to help."

Jerome had handed her the ether mask and the can. Then he was smearing his right hand and forearm with sterile petroleum jelly. His crimped hand disappeared into the woman.

"My God, that's good. She's dilated to beat the band, and she's not bleeding much. But I need contractions."

"I'll do it," the girl said, taking the ampules from Edna. The woman stiffened at the ammonia.

"I've got the baby," Jerome said. They could see his hand moving inside the woman's belly.

"Tell her to help me, to push," Jerome told the girl. Edna watched the girl speak to the woman, watched her belly ripple and her lips whiten with the effort.

"It's turning, thank God, it's turning," Jerome said. He knelt between the woman's legs, head off to the side, his arm up in her like Edna had seen the preacher do with cows. She felt a sudden twinge of nausea. Blood trickled down Jerry's arm.

"Turning, turning, by God, there, there, look by God," and he withdrew his hand. Edna peeked. Was that its head, that wrinkled black thing? The girl looked, too, unflinching at her mother's vagina, swollen, open, bleeding.

"Now, she's got to help," Jerome hollered. "Got to, or we'll have to cut her open. Cut her open like a hog. Tell her that. Tell her we don't want that. Tell her we need her strength."

The girl spoke louder to her mother, pulling on one of her braids. The Indian man came to look over Edna's shoulder, grunted and went back to his corner and whiskey.

"The ampules," Jerry told Edna, and she snapped another under the woman's nose, and then Jerry leaned over the woman and slapped her hard across the mouth. The woman's eyes flew open.

"Shove, goddam it," he swore. "Push or you'll die and the baby will, too. Shove!" And he hit her again. The girl's eyes widened in shock, then narrowed as she understood. Now the woman labored in earnest, her eyes angry, her mouth open, the bite stick pushed aside and her cries of terror and fear and pain echoing in the smoky, smelly cabin. Jerome heard the shaman commence a drum-like chant. Boom-thud-boom-thud.

"Coming, here it comes. Coming," exclaimed Jerry, and Edna saw him reach again into the woman, this time with the big spoon forceps she'd boiled, and then the baby's head appeared out of the woman in the forceps, and Jerry gently removed them. Edna saw the creases the forceps left on the wrinkled, copper-and-black skull. Jerry had the baby's shoulders now, and with a tug the buttocks and legs appeared, trailing the umbilical cord. Jerry's forefinger went to the infant's mouth, pried it open and swiped out mucus. He blew frantically in it, and with a cotton swab cleared out the nose. He turned the baby upside down.

The smacks rang through the cabin. One of the smaller children started to wail, and then Edna and the rest heard the thin cry of the newborn, and Jerry smiled.

"Look at that," he said, holding the baby head-up. "Just look at that, will you, a little girl, and alive as can be." The Indian man grunted again. The girl held her mother's head up to see, but Edna detected no reaction. Jerry handed up the baby.

"Edna, wash her off, will you, and find something to wrap her in."

Edna did, with the girl's help, while Jerry cut the umbilicus now with the surgical scissors, then quickly sutured the stem. He dabbed carbolic acid on the sutures. Then he delivered the placenta and stitched up the woman, carefully washing her and using the antiseptic. The girl brought him a clean rag for a sanitary napkin. He soaked the carbolic into it and placed it on the woman, who now lay still as if she were dead, except for the steady heaving of her chest. The infant squirmed in Edna's arms.

"Give her the baby," Jerome said, and Edna saw how weary he looked now, standing in the room's center, the color drained from his face, his hands trembling. Old, Lord, he looked almost old, lots older than twenty-four.

"You can let them in, now," Jerome said. The girl jabbered to the father, who threw open the door. The women boiled in first, to crowd around the pallet, and the shaman danced over, still chanting.

"Thank you, doctor. You saved both lives," the girl said.

"You helped," Jerry told her. "And we were lucky. You tell your mother to keep clean, and take care of the baby. And not to have any more for a while. No intercourse, no braves, for two months. You understand? No men. Will you tell her that?"

Edna noticed the girl's mouth tighten, and her dark eyes narrow. She was pretty in a way, this Indian girl. Slim, with a longer face than most Sioux, but with their born-in dignified bearing.

"She didn't want more, doctor. The girl stopped."

"I see," Jerome said, looking at the father, standing expressionless in the corner. "Then tell her no men for six months. Doctor's orders. And tell her to come see me. We can talk about not having babies."

Edna stiffened. Jerry was Catholic. He'd never mentioned, what was the ten-dollar word, contraception, to her, and here she was, probably pregnant, and not much older than this girl.

"I never want babies," the girl suddenly blurted out. "Never." She shook her long black braids violently.

"You'll get over that," Jerry said, "but at your age, if you mean it, come see me. I'll introduce you to the pessary, or pisser, if you like." He looked square at Edna. "Darling, let's go home."

The girl called in Lakota to her father. He nodded, and she called again. The son appeared from outside, and motioned that they were to come. Jerome took a last look at the woman, who seemed to be sleeping propped up against a squaw, the infant pulling at her breast. He shrugged into his coat, and helped Edna with hers. Then they were in the cold, on the buckboard. The moon had nearly set, but the wind had laid, too. They rode with arms around each other. Their house felt deliciously warm. Edna forsook her bath, settling for a warm washup. When she crawled beneath the comforter, Jerome was half-asleep. Another day for her surprise. But she itched with a question.

"Jerry," she asked. "Why did you mention that birth-control thing? I thought you Catholics liked babies, and big families."

He smiled, his eyes half-open.

"I do for us. For people who want them, can afford them."

"And the Indians?"

"You saw. The way they're kept, they're like brutes in a breeding ground."

"Come now. Maybe not like us, but they're people, too, aren't they?"

But she saw he was fast asleep.

V

Serengeti

T hey had come to see the big cats and their son, who was
himself like a big cat—restless, wary, spooky. They had
also come to save what they could of themselves, if anything was
salvageable, in the hope—as she thought—that in the wreckage
of lives, human and otherwise, here they might find their bad
compass point. Now the rains pelted on the tents. The sensible
big cats would be in the brush, or under the lower acacias and
baobabs, sheltering from the elements, including Land Rovers
and camera-bearers, all the post-Hemingway joke that Africa
had become.

Their son sat on his porch at the adjacent tent, strumming
a pack guitar they'd given him as a wedding gift five years ago.
Just inside the circle of camp-lantern light stood Joseph, the
Masai guard-boy who had been drawn from his rounds by the
Appalachian tunes. He annoyed her, the boy did, stiffly proud,
pandering to their son for a big tip tomorrow when they would
have to leave without seeing the big cats. She sipped the last of
her third gin-and-tonic, put the glass on the brass-bound camp
table. So much faux-period luxury in these stationary safari

camps, a convenient bush-plane ride from Nairobi or Dar es Salaam. They ate their big breakfast, returned in the cars for a four-course lunch, bounced around in the cars in a post-prandial penance, then returned for the five-course supper served by the obliging staff who doubled as native dancers for the evening's entertainment. If she'd been Mrs. McComber, she'd have killed them all, not just her feckless husband, now making his unreadable notes in their tent. Well, he was at least an amiable alcoholic who did no more than she to discourage their son, who expected more of his parents than he did of himself.

Actually, she wished her husband would finish his notes and come through the tent's fly to kiss her and hand her another drink. She wished her son would stop strumming, ever since he was small a defense against stress. She didn't expect either.

"Joseph, come closer," her son called to the Masai. The boy advanced, clutching his *runga*, his red toga dripping onto the porch. "Here," her son said, "take it. Just hold it and bring your fingers over the strings. Here."

———

He remembered them when they were all young, him a boy and his parents in middle-age mini-godness, like semi-demi-hemi quavers, fast and graceful, almost too swift to be played. These days they seemed like half-notes, squatted on a score neither they nor he could read. Their plane was at two tomorrow afternoon. Maybe some last-chance cats would be out. His shortwave said the rain would stop. He looked again at his mother ignoring the wailing Joseph made. Still pretty in a worn way. Still incapable of knowing him for anything other than a son. Oh, and now his father had come out, waving across the rain. He waved back. His father now grown stout and intermittently silly. They'd want him to come over for a drink, and he would. He'd explain about the improving weather. They'd go to dinner, sheltered by Joseph's gigantic red umbrella, like a mega-sized Travelers Insurance ad. Both of them would be upbeat, and not entirely falsely. He knew they hadn't had a bad time. Seen the impala, the buffaloes, the hippo, the great and small gazelles, the jackals and hyenas and baboons and giraffes and elephant after elephant. Shot hundreds of pictures for the in-laws and family back home.

"I cannot play, Bwana." He felt the guitar come into his hands and looked at Joseph. In the rain, it seemed he was crying.

"Coming over, Mom! Dad!" he called. Joseph popped open the big umbrella.

"Bwana mind the rain," the boy said.

"Joseph, I'm not Bwana, just a hotel guest." He didn't add that that honorific pleased him in some vestigial playacting way. They stepped off the tent's porch into the steady rain. To their left, the river roared, one of the few waterways coursing this part of the great plain. Come August the wildebeest and zebra would ford it by the thousands as they traveled their ancient impulse to come north for food, copulation, maybe just a change of scene. All along the route the big cats—cheetah, lion, leopard—would watch with yellow-eyed surety for the young, the old, the weak or wounded. Some of the migrants would drown, wash up to rot in the unforgiving sun, not unlike the corpses this part of the world seemed to grow as regularly as maize. In his job as a journalist, he'd seen more than enough of them, enough so that whenever the vexations of normal life came calling, like bills or marital disputes or child-rearing questions, he could shunt them to some siding of concern or perversely, devote all his attention to them, repressing the visions of bodies burning in pyres, of mass graves, of the bloated corpses bobbing at water's edge, the crocodiles' breakfast. He counted 36 steps to his parent's tent, as many as he had years.

"Hi," he said. "A sundowner and then supper?" Joseph snapped shut the umbrella, then retreated to hunker in the farthest corner. His mother tilted her head toward his father, an echo of a grace note in the gesture.

"Jerry, could you do the drinks, please?"

—— — —— ——

Most of the ice cubes hadn't survived, but he didn't mind. He drank a mouthful straight from the bottle before pouring into the jigger. Three nice clean glasses, nicely and cleanly set out on the brass-bound bar. Tonic at hand. Rain doing its pattering on the plasticized-canvas roof. Lovely mosquito netting draped on the lovely four-poster bed to which, once in his prime, he'd have tied a lady love but certainly not Alice, whose bright patter to their son Josh sped syllable by syllable to him through the tent flap. She'd always been far too straight for that, the sort of woman who trades virginity for (a) children, and (b) financial security. Anything else was gravy and too fattening. He poured the tonic. The bitter aroma rose to remind him of his failures. Not in procreation. He'd done well in that, albeit with too many rehearsals for Alice's taste, both in and out of wedlock. No, his failure was in selling himself too cheap—to employers, to his family, above all to booze. He couldn't even be a big-league drunk. Instead he plodded along drinking too much for health and too little for either enlightenment or ennui. True, the alcohol had lubricated the high times of their young-married stage, the parties and the travel on trust funds and the bright, brittle companionship they'd courted, everyone with a drink in hand and a bon mot or bonbon or both in mouth. He supposed that would be what Josh remembered best about his parents, especially here in the Serengeti where the night sounds of hunting cats and the bright equatorial moon cast an exotic spell dissipated only partly by the sunrise, promptly at 7:06 every morning.

"Dad? Drinks? And we're due for supper soon."

His son's familiar command—"Is supper ready yet? Have you looked at my homework?"—roused him. Even if long ago he'd given in to self-pity and recrimination, he recognized bullshit when it walked the trails. He hadn't been that bad, and neither had Alice. The kids were a wash: the one thing he knew about children was that each saw the phenomena of their lives with the same jaundice he saw his. Self-justification was the human condition. Without it no sex, no war, no art, no politics, no love, no pity, no irony, no philosophy, no science, *y nada y pues nada y nada y nada. Our father who art in nada* and so on as the old African fraud had written. And so Josh could call for drink, just as his sister and brother could to another waiter while they, probably, dined at San Francisco's *embarcadero* with tony ad-agency friends.

He clinked the glasses, then balanced two in his right hand, holding onto his more fortified one with his left. The rain seemed to have diminished, but that only made the river's roar louder. He remembered once in a case when the courtroom fell silent and his stomach rumbled so loudly a bailiff came running toward a presumed disturbance. Physical nonevidence, he reckoned that. With the padded shoulder of his safari jacket leading, he pushed through the tent flap.

"Drinks, anyone," he said. Their smiles were perfunctory, and he remembered, too late, that he hadn't offered the Masai boy anything.

───

Joseph smelled the leopard in the moist air. She would come tonight. The *mzungu* assembled would see her and not understand her, as they saw all this and understood nothing. He understood more, in English, in Swahili, in his native tongue, than they. He liked the son, but if that son were in his village he would not be allowed to denigrate his parents, even in his thoughts. He would not believe the Great World circled him because it was the other way. All the people merely stood on the great belt of the earth as guests and ran its ways until they could come back to the beginning. That was why his people and their cousins the Samburo and the various peoples of the great lake named after the white people's queen and the Turku people far to the north could run so far, seeming not to breathe, and bring home the gold and money from those who could not so run. He looked at the diners, some still puffing from the short walk to the big-tent eating place where they would eat their impala that was sometimes only goat and drink the good wines from the south and say what they had seen today like the animals were on the television sets he had seen when he and his father took their cattle to the shipping place for the sale in Nairobi, which his father said was only a made-up place, the stop for the railroad that had nothing to do with the paths the people had ever run. At home with his people, they would eat real impala and drink the fermented blood and milk. He could at last see the girl he would marry. He had known her all his life but seen her only once, yet he ached for her, as did those of the big cats, during the time when they had to mate. He knew that humans were the same. The big man who drank too much still loved and ached for the woman who drank too much. The son has his love, too, back in Nairobi, but could not see the great rift, like the valley of the plain itself, that separated those who had given him birth. They could not see the long paths, Joseph thought. Not one of those he'd served saw the long ways of the earth and the great belt and its people. They believed in machines and roads. They would not understand his uncle's son who had walked away from the job Joseph now did, walked over the plain through the night to his home, through the big cats and animals, so that he could attend his mother's burial. "Only three days," his cousin had said. So he had walked, not on the roads, not in a machine, carrying only his *runga* and a pouch of dried cow-meat.

The diners' second course had arrived, the impala, and the rain had stopped. The moon lit a passing cloud. Joseph looked at the river from the overhanging porch between the dining tent and the water. Across was the tree where the leopard would come. Thankfully he and his tribesmen would not have to dance tonight. It was the third night and they only had to dance the lion dance on the second and fourth, so he could now come close to the table from which he would get his money and listen to the white people. He did not mind the white people. They were only different, but they wanted so much that he could not understand. He wanted only his marriage, and the family that would come, a large repayment for his large dowry—ten cows, all he had earned as a herdsman from the age of ten, eating the dust of the cars as they scarred the plain, but enough for a good wife and a *banda* and sons like himself to carry on.

"So, Dad, you like the impala?" the music-making son asked.

"It's good, like venison."

"It *is* venison, really, isn't it," the wife said. "Aren't antelopes deer?"

"Well," the father said, "they're ungulates anyway. I don't know if they're from the same family."

"They're not," the son said. "Deer are from the family *cervidae* and antelopes are the family *bovidae*, like cows."

"How in hell do you know that?" the father asked.

"That fancy university you sent me to. When you wanted me to be a doctor I took comparative anatomy and part of that was taxonomy."

"Your father thinks comparative anatomy means screwing," the wife said. "Let's have another beer."

Joseph watched her wave at his friend Richard, who was table-waiting tonight. The big brown bottles of beer would come cold from the refrigerator. After the whites had gone to bed, when there were only the night sounds, he and Richard and the others drank theirs straight from the case, and laughed and joked and talked about girls, speaking Masai and calling one another by their tribal names, not the missionary ones. That was real, with the moon always in the same place at the same time, like the great herds that came up in August, always on time.

But here on the dining terrace all seemed false, like the festival masks. The whites chattering like the blue monkeys of the coast, using the English words that had no meaning for him. If an impala was like something else, what did it matter? Now the father and mother were barking at one another while the son looked out across the river. Animals, too, did that. The *simbas* roared and cuffed and wrestled sometimes while their cubs watched or played, but they soon tired of it and took naps or walked away. His father and his wives often barked, too, but never long. There was too much to do, and there always was the beer or neighbors or the wind-up radio to go to. Only a good feud with the lake people deserved real anger.

"I'm going down to the river," the son said, pushing back from the table. The father and mother stopped barking to watch him go. Then they pushed back and followed, taking the big beer bottles. Joseph knew the son did not want to listen any more and had gone to see if the leopard would come.

Alice wondered why, no matter the situation, that she always was behind the men. Josh and Jerry crowded the railing, and she could see only through the space between their shoulders. Across the river the leopard tree stood stark against the night sky. The equatorial nights bothered her. They were dark enough, but there seemed always to be a residual light somewhere, like the faint shadow on a double-exposed negative. Close enough to life, she supposed. The son she'd borne now lived as a free-floating radical, out of her orbit, and the husband she'd once loved could not now love her more than the alcohol that ran his life. For that matter, it was possible that she had not loved either of them as her parents had taught her love should be, as in the books, lifelong and immutable. If nothing else Africa had showed her up close what everyone at some root base knew: we all stalk, kill, and eat something, not out of malice, but from genetic, maybe even social, necessity. Whichever, the results were nourishment, progeny, waste.

"Alice! Look! A croc!"

Her husband's hand pulled at her elbow. With an uncharacteristically decisive motion, he propelled her to a space between Josh and him. Below in the dark roiling water she could make out the snout projected like a little surfboard studded by dark eyes. The reptile held firm against the current. She could imagine its short, powerful legs ruddering against the flow, and she wondered if it were hungry. She felt Jerry lean against her, heard her son cry something, and then behind her a light came on, a bright limelight, and across the river, roaring now like an animal, she saw the leopard emerge from the brush, deliberately as a moonrise, its quatrefoil paws marking the soft mud of the river bank, its back arched only a vertebrae or two, advancing on the tree. Her intaken breath corresponded with those of the diners, of Jerry and Josh, seemingly of the night itself.

The leopard stalked the tree, threw its powerful self up to the nearest crotch where, she saw, a cache of meat had been stored. Fastidiously, the leopard pawed the man-given treat, ripping open the cotton net that held the prey, then settled down in the blue-white light to eat, while cameras and videocams recorded the great hunt. Alice turned away from the rail to see Joseph smiling broadly, looking at her but past her and over the rail and past the leopard out into the equatorial night, and she felt a tug she had not felt of too long.

"Mom, isn't it something?" her son said. She smelled the irony. Beside her, Jerry held the game-watching binocs glued to his eyes. A murmur bubbled up from the river when a piece of uneaten impala hit the disturbed water. The leopard chewed like any house cat, happy for its meal, uncaring about those who watched it. The new moon, sharp as a fingernail, cast a backlight on the leopard, the river, the dining porch, and she saw when turning around, the boy Joseph who stood in quiet majesty back by the bar, in his red toga and red-mud streaked hair, holding his *runga*, looking at her, she thought. A shriek from somewhere in the brush tore her attention back to the leopard, who looked up, around, then dragged the bait meat back down the tree. She slipped out of arc light's ring like a shadow passing the moon's slivered surface.

"Mom! Look!"

Her son's voice seemed to come from twenty years ago, when he'd bring homework to show her, but now he tugged at her, pointed toward the leopard tree. Slinking out of the darkness, muzzle high, came a silver-backed hyena. It regarded the leopards' perch for a moment while the cameras whirred and churned, then followed the leopard's spoor into the blackness. Behind her the tourists chirruped, and she found herself joining them, the exclamations, the what-about-thats, the wondering if it had been the hyena's mate who shrieked or something else, something else following the baited predator that held the carrion.

"We go now," came Joseph's voice at her side.

"It's beautiful," she said to her son. "Too beautiful."

"Eating and being eaten?" her husband said. "What's new? And so Joseph, you escort us back now, and all will be well?"

"Yes, Bwana," Joseph said. She did not know exactly to whom he spoke, her son or her husband, but he raised his stick and pointed, as if the three of them were cattle to be herded.

⸻

The river's rise threatened to come over the bank, but the rain had stopped, so now the rushing water's only menace was in its sound. Clouds still danced around the piece of moon, around which a circle showed. Trick of the atmosphere, like what you saw around the sodium arcs in Nairobi or New York or Paris or Hong Kong or anywhere that technology had touched. Inside his parents' tent the gas lantern cast them into silhouette, the shadows making the moves familiar to him for so many years: the donning of nightwear, the ceremonial toast with their last drink, his father picking up a book, his mother slumping into the camp chair to study the photographs from their past week in Nairobi, of him and his wife and son and the servants and the house. Those images, he knew, pleased her more than would sighting the big cats.

With the camp's electricity shut off for the night, there seemed to be a corresponding quiet from the man-made intrusions. He heard the river, the little scuffling that always seemed to come from the bush, and from across the river the crash of something large moving away across the ridge. True, not all was natural. He heard his father's snoring, his mother's shuffle through the photos. From the dining tent he could hear faint laughs and a Masai flute. Joseph might be there, or maybe out on his rounds. Although the camp was fenced, except at the river, nothing could hold back the creatures if they came. This morning, before the cars, they'd seen elephants and buffaloes ten meters from the gate moving as some poet had said, "in their major freedom." Joseph had said when the elephants came to his village there was nothing to do but stay away or kill them and the white men had made that a sin.

The lantern blinked out in his parents' tent. He remembered his boyhood, the camping at some or another Corps of Engineers lake, and the same kind of lanterns and the same vague excitement and fear at being out in some other species' dominion. The wonderful wood smoke, too, and the underdone camp food, and the sunburned frenzy of returning home, things he'd never have again. He yawned. Tomorrow maybe his mother would see the big cats, and if not, she'd still have had her safari and she could dine out on the stories. His father took the Thoreau route: if you've seen a house cat you have the idea of all cats so why see more? But that was conditioned by the drink and the self-loathing and cynicism it bred. Still, he could see them in the bush plane, maybe the Otter, back to Nairobi, sitting side by side, contesting each other's experience but taking it all in, the Serengeti, the Great Rift, the Ngong hills where Karen Blixen had failed as a coffee farmer and succeeded as a writer and where Denys Finch-Hatton, her lover, was buried. They'd take pictures out the windows, and turn to take one of him in his bush jacket, looking very foreign correspondenty, and he'd know that their life and his was just like this, a journey with the hopes of reaching somewhere, finding something, a glimpse of big cats or a leopard tree or the long face of a Masai boy or themselves, all just a trek, and that their salvation lay only in the hope of it.

He stumbled in the dark getting up from the tent porch's chair. The flap unzipping seemed to shred the air, but then he was inside and the bed was near. He tossed his jacket and shirt and shorts in the direction of the bureau. They hit his guitar, and he wondered at the foreign strained sound as it rolled out across the great plain.

Nairobi

Nelson was asleep again at his post, while the radio blared an odd blend of vaguely African music and American pops. Watching Nelson, though, he understood the impulse. Sleep away the dark hours, make sure no one broke through the gates, rake up leaves when otherwise not occupied, get your salary from the rich Americans, and go home to your shack. Seeing Nelson from the second-floor bedroom, he certainly understood. Here, safely imprisoned in his son's house, he watched, too. Items of the dawn. The house stood silent. The maids asleep in their quarters in the little house. His son and daughter-in-law asleep in their wide bed. His wife dead to the world in the bed he'd just vacated. All was well, down to the iron-barred windows, scrolled to look like spiderwebs, and the locked gate leading up to these sleeping quarters that he had to quietly unlock so that he could go down to be by himself and have a morning beer.

The being by himself was actually more important than anything. He'd retired from a liver-killing advertising job. He pretended to write prose, an endeavor that his son found amusing, in the British sense. His wife had long ago given up on him and her and everything, as their adventures in the Serengeti and on the Mombasa coast had taught him. So, now, before the servants arose and Nelson turned off his radio, he had the chance to tiptoe down the stairs, unlock the upstairs gate (a relic of the Mau-Mau era) and stare out through the spider-scroll windows at more gated houses and a future he couldn't imagine. So the beer tasted fresh, and the laptop keys felt familiar. But what could he say?

He typed, "Being of sound mind..." and then stopped. That statement certainly could be debated. He backspaced it away, took a swig of the Tusker beer. Hemingway had said just write one true sentence and go from there. He typed, "Things are fucked up. Fubared. Snafued. Whose fault?" He did wonder. Upstairs all the sleepers lay, seemingly at peace. Outside, Nelson's radio still played, its blare muffled by the thick walls. He could hear stirrings in the servants' quarters. Soon Anna the cook and Mary the nanny would appear. He hurried to the pantry for another Tusker, returning to the laptop to stare at the one true sentence. What was the most important part? The fuckedupness or the fault? Did it matter? From the kitchen came the soft footfall of Mary, who competed with the cook and the chauffeur for the affections of her charge, his grandson. She would count the new empties in the Tusker case, wish him good morning, and preempt some of Anna's duties by making the tea, preparing the bread for toast, laying out the jams and marmalades and yogurt. Anna would supplement with eggs and bacon if anyone wanted them.

The one true sentence glared at him. Fubar. Snafu. Fault. So what? One man's fubar might be another's road to riches and fame, or to a job like Nelson's out by the gatehouse listening to Metallica or his son's tony reporting job or his wife's drink-raddled University post or any of a hundred passages to the side of riches and fame that occupied any person until blue-eyed Mister Death made his call. Perhaps, too, there was no such thing as fault, and hence no such thing as guilt. Perhaps relativity and situation ruled. From the kitchen drifted the odor of frying bacon. He shook the Tusker bottle. Empty. He couldn't risk Anna and Mary's eyes following him into the pantry. He put the laptop to sleep, deciding he'd stow it upstairs, get into some proper clothes complete with a stashed half-pint of vodka and take a walk.

Just past the iron Mau Mau gate the riser groaned under his weight. He stood for a moment to see if he'd awakened anybody but heard nothing except a faint snore. He shifted the laptop to his right hand so he could hold the railing. He walked close to it, where the boards didn't creak. At the top, he turned right a few steps, then right again into his and his wife's room. She slept on her left side, turned away from the depression where his body had been and toward the iron spiderwebbed windows. The fine bones of her face, the brown hair streaked with gray, called to him from long ago, but he knew better than to answer. He put the laptop into the closet before easing his cargo pants and safari shirt and jacket off the hangars. Into his left hand went his boots, socks stuffed in them. From the raised dressing table he took his knife, wallet, coins, and fresh underwear. He'd dress in the bathroom. He stopped on his tiptoeing exit to fetch a fresh half-pint of vodka from his sacrosanct briefcase.

"Good morning, *bwana*," Nelson said, shoving open the heavy iron gate.

"Good morning, Nelson," he replied. "Off for a stroll."

"Good, good, *bwana*."

He stepped onto the heavily rutted red-dirt and gravel road, turning right, toward an intersection with an equally rutted road. Daniel Arap Moi's priorities did not extend to infrastructure, although the Kenyan president did keep the highways to his various palatial homes in good order. The morning air chilled him, here at 6,700 feet above sea level. Close to the equator, too, so that the mean daytime temperature was around 75 Fahrenheit falling as low as 30 degrees at night sometimes. Now the sun stood three fingers above the eastern horizon. Today might be hot, up in the eighties and at this altitude, enervating. He turned at the intersection, heading for the macadam road that eventually led to the city center. When he reached it, he joined the line of black workers who trudged in from their shanty towns each day to work as gardeners or day labor in the city or to open one of the roadside sheds or *dukas* that sold cloth, kabobs, furniture, flowers, chickens, bleeding slabs of meat, old appliances of every kind, faux African artifacts of every stripe. By the sheds, often in rows in squatter bazaars, the merchants laughed and drank beer, occasionally whistling at passing cars to stop to examine the wares. Most were male, most were young.

He noticed the almost rhythmic manner of their walking this morning, as if they were an armed force on a mission. Many of the women carried baskets on their heads, or slings of sticks for firewood on their backs, bending them into inverted Ls. The men carried bundles, too, probably containing lunch or a spare shirt or a piece of plastic for the frequent afternoon rains. He carried only what fit in the many pockets of his safari clothes, one of which did hold a plastic anorak. Their column approached an intersection. To the left a half-mile lay a flossy shopping center where his son and family shopped in safe comfort, and ate wraps or Thai food while his grandson cavorted in the center's play area. Immediately in front of him, in the green middle of the traffic circle, the carvers had their wares displayed. *Makonde* they were called, he remembered from his Swahili phrase book. At least he'd studied that a bit since the Serengeti safari and the time in Mombasa. He dodged a Land Rover and stepped onto the grass. The three men, one at work on a nearly life-size reclining lion, glanced his way, then back to work or to scanning the passing cars for potential customers. They were more than accustomed to costumed foreign white people, especially here by the shopping center, beyond which to the north lay the hallowed rich lands of Muthaiga. Only the wealthy—foreign diplomats, cronies of Moi, businessmen, bankers and other thieves—lived there. Since 1913 there'd been a Muthaiga club surrounded by walled homes. In the old days, it was said, Muthaiga reeked of white Bohemian highjinks and money; now it seemed just to emit the universal odor of wealth. His son told him there'd been a word coined for the new rich of Muthaiga: *wa Benzi,* for all the Mercedes-Benz cars the liberated black bureaucrats owned.

"*Bwana,* you like the *duma?*"

The lilting voice at his elbow chased the guidebook thoughts away. He saw he'd been staring, unseeing, at a carved three-quarters size standing cheetah.

"Yes, very well done."

"Would you like to purchase it?" the man asked. He looked middle aged, but was probably, like Nelson, in his thirties and probably, like Nelson, a Kikiyu. He wore a blue collarless Indian shirt above an East African skirt, the *kikoi,* this one in black and gray stripes. No doubt for effect. Most Kenyans in the cities dressed in Western clothes.

"No, thank you, but it's beautifully done."

"Yes. You are American?"

"Yes.

"Very rich, America. I would like to go one day."

"I hope you can."

"Yes. Perhaps you can help me if I come there. Would you give me your name, *bwana?*"

He could find no guile in the man's eyes. Extraordinary that so many believed a stranger, an American, might help them.

"My name, yes, my name, " he found himself saying, then more surprising, fumbling in his wallet for his defunct business card. He thrust it at the man.

"*Asante sana,*" the man burbled. "Perhaps I will see you again in America."

"Yes, perhaps."

He moved past the man, through the many Makonde toward the line of walkers headed for the city center. He wondered what the man would do with his card, the useless totem from a *mzungu*. Could he even read it? Would he keep it? Burn it? Leave it with the other trash accumulated in the traffic circle, the chips wrappers and paper cups and wood shavings? And why would he want it when he must know he would never get to America and if he did, wouldn't find this former ad man. A passport scheme? Well, no matter.

The sun stood higher, warming his back. A few hundred yards on there was a strip mall with a bank, a grocery, a liquor store, some clothes shops, the inevitable curio stands and shops, a butcher, a bank. He could also get a *matatu* there, one of the infernal, over-packed jitneys that pulled up blaring popular music at jet-plane decibels. Quite uncomfortable and smelly, but cheap and efficient. He'd observed that the official surface transport system worked sporadically at best. There always seemed to be a holiday or a strike for those workers. His son had told him that Nairobians only worked when they wanted to, which was why it was good the household had a chauffeur to drive and a cook to shop. No doubt by now that household was up and bustling, probably wondering where he was. Well, Nelson knew he'd gone for a stroll.

With a dozen fellow trudgers, he turned off into the small mall, fairly nicely arranged, with a courtyard surrounded by the shops. The ATM machine was built into the outer wall of the closed bank. A security guard with assault rifle leaned near it. He inserted his card, pushed in his PIN and prayed. The machine whirred, grunted, and amazingly produced $200 worth of schillings, or *shilingi*. He wished the liquor store was open, but he had his vodka still intact. Spurred by the thought, he approached a *duka* stationed by the road.

"*Pombe*," he told the turbaned woman. He took the cool Tusker and swigged. This woman also sold various sizes of carved giraffes, along with kites, roasted corn, bedraggled flowers, and cheap plastic toys that had China written all over them. He felt at ease, watching the increasing flow of traffic. No fubar, no snafu, no fault. Why was that? Just a change of scene?

Back there his troubled wife still existed, and his burdened son and daughter-in-law and his innocent grandson and, of course, like the early morning ground mist, his own clouded existence, loveless and useless, possessed only by a dream that dispossessed him and an addiction that did the same. What was it the poet Lowell had said, "I, myself, am hell"?

He handed over the big brown Tusker bottle and took another. So what? Just now, he felt fine. A flame tree waved bright scarlet blooms at him from across the road. He stood near a jacaranda tree and a healthy bougainvillea vine. The last of the second beer gurgled down. He heard the four-cylinder roar of an unmuffled engine, so he moved to the battered sign that marked the *matatu's* official stop. Actually, they stopped wherever the *quat*-crazed driver pleased or where a passenger demanded with a small bribe.

The chugging jitney pounded to a stop. Three women and two men erupted from it while almost simultaneously he and two men shouldered into the rank seats. Another man rode the running board as they peeled out toward the heart of the city. He clung to a seat back, jammed in a half-stoop between the bench seats, just now occupied by, in front of him, two enormous black women and a small child, and behind him—their knees against his torso—three Masai-skinny men with a chicken. With a shudder and clatter the *matatu* collapsed at its next stop, the shopping center nearest the city, this one still under construction with cranes delivering concrete panels to levels where shops already had opened, forcing shoppers to dodge the workmen and incoming loads of material. The skinny men scrambled off, so he fell onto the seat nearest the side-opening that served as entrance and exit and also a departure point for anyone who didn't hold on tight. The jitney bolted forward in a great exhalation of black smoke and they were on Kenyatta Avenue, joining an ever-growing stream of *wa Benzis*, trucks, carts, automobiles, motor scooters and motor bikes, and the *boda-bodas*, the bicycle taxis that were even more lethal than the *matatus*. They careened past a Shell station, an old hotel rumored to be populated by untrustworthy Middle Eastern visitors, past yet another atriumed shopping mall featuring a fine Indian restaurant where his son had taken them to eat, then past the Masai market and a turnoff toward the venerable Norfolk Hotel of *Out of Africa* fame.

The running-board riders—there were three now—disembarked. The violent left turn toward the City Market threw him against a stolid Asian man who smelled of cheese, beer and sweat. Then they lurched to a stop by the market teeming with morning customers. He scrambled out, realizing he could hardly hear, so loud had been the Euro- and Ameripop blasts. He stood, gathering himself and wondering at the people, many in traditional dress, who clogged the two-story market, buying fruits, vegetables, animal flesh, plastic goods, bolts of cloth, stove kerosene, rope, the occasional wood or plastic toy. Intermixed weaved the camera-laden tourists, bent on buying masks, colorful clothes they'd never wear, wall hangings of animals and natives, bright handwoven rugs, and the ubiquitous Makonde of animals and Giacometti-slender Masai and their cousins, the Samburu.

"*Hatari! Hatari!*" came shouting into his ears, displacing the jitney bedlam. Someone pushed him to the side, out of the path of a speeding motorcycle. Flustered and sweaty, he looked for whomever had warned him of the danger, but the crowd's flow continued and so did the traffic. Fubar, snafu, his fault? He pushed his way onto the sidewalk, heading for Biashara Street where the Indians and other Asians made a killing. A shop window stuffed with animal carvings halted him. Was that it? He felt that electric surge when an idea struck him fully, unfortunately too seldom in advertising or writing. He shook his head and idled on. The bend into Biashara Street brought him into another throng of Kenyans and tourists, popping in and out of the shoe stores, safari and trinket emporia, dry goods purveyances, snack stands and bucket-shop travel agents. He headed for the sign that said Harari's Stamp Shot Ltd., where at his son's suggestion he'd bought the safari clothes. Harari's sold stamps for collections, and *kikois*, shirts, hats, Kenyan flags to match all the others or the world, the requisite carvings and mementoes, socks, sneakers, raw cloth and camping gear.

The Asians waved as if they knew him. He thought they might have remembered him as the man who turned down the zip-off cargo pants/shorts as being too difficult to manage.

"So, sir, you desire something? May I help you?"

The soft voice emanating from a roundish, soft brown face soothed after the clamor of the hip-hop jitney ride and the market-district streets. He felt again a nanosecond of frisson and he thought he knew what it meant.

"Yes, please. I'd like to have a throwaway camera. And I want to look at hats and a knife."

The camera came easily, a 27-exposure Kodak with flash. The hats he narrowed to two: a broad-brimmed white-hunter number and a baseball-style cap with a long bill, like Hemingway used fishing. He chose that in the usual khaki.

"And you said, sir, you desired a knife?"

"Yes. A hunting knife."

Such items the host kept in a locked case in a tiny room at the rear of the store, reached by pushing through a beaded curtain.

"Here, a fine selection."

He surveyed the fine selection. They ranged in length from six inches to ten or twelve, some with both edges honed, others with single cutting edges, a few with serrated back edges, like a U.S. Marine killing knife. A couple of machetes also lay on the black cotton. He'd noticed they sold such things in grocery stores here, which was not illogical. Most men and women worked at least part time in fields, either their own garden patches or some farmer's. Weeds grew prodigiously everywhere, and God knew the machete was an effective tool. You had to look no further than Rwanda, Burundi and whatever they called Zaire these days. But he felt he wanted something with a sheath, something less peasanty. He pointed to a sturdy twelve-inch blade with a stabbing hilt.

"That one, please."

"Ah, of course, of course. A good choice."

An expensive one, too, he found, even in schillings. He put the items on his Visa, put on his cap keeping the camera and knife in a plastic sack, and prepared himself for the brilliant sunlight in the street. The genial Asian accompanied him to the doorway.

"So, now you are ready for an adventure."

"Well, yes, I think so. Thank you."

"And thanks to you, sir. May your day go well."

So polite, these people who with the Arabs occupied the small-entrepreneur rung in Kenyan society. That was a moral step up, though, from the nineteenth century role of some Asians and many Arabs as slave traders. He fitted his sunglasses and stepped forward. The sun bore down even more than he'd expected, as did the crowd of shoppers. A woman swathed in a gold and brown dashiki wove past, a basket of cabbages and plantains balanced on her head while she perused the English language *Daily Nation*. He set off toward the large north-south road, Moi Avenue. His new cap deflected the heat downward so that he saw shimmers before his glasses. Near the end of Biashara Street, he saw the sign he wanted. "Day Tours," it proclaimed. He pushed by some men chewing *quat* and through a beaded curtain into the scent of cinnamon incense. The greeting here emanated from a squat black man with faint ritual scars on his cheeks and the missing lower-front teeth characteristic of the Luo people. His son had told him the extractions were part of old initiation ceremonies and had the added benefit of allowing straw-feeding in the event of lockjaw, often epidemic near Lake Victoria where the Luo homeland lay.

"*Jambo*," the man said.

"*Jambo*. I'm inquiring about day tours."

"Yes, yes. Please sit here."

The man settled behind a worn wooden desk, shoving scattered papers to the side.

"A day tour? You want something like the Karen Blixen Museum and the things of Langata, the *bomas*, the Giraffe Center, the Bird Sanctuary? Very nice, very popular. Very close to Nairobi, all in a car with driver."

He'd enjoyed the Blixen place when his daughter-in-law had taken him and his wife there. *Out of Africa* vibrated there for him, and he could almost picture Blixen, a.k.a. Isaak Dinesen listening hard for the sound of Denys Finch-Hatton's plane as she waited, like so many white colonialists, for the fates and the black folks to bring them in a bumper coffee or tea crop. He'd seen their remnants when his family had visited the Norfolk Hotel's Lord Delamere Bar. The giraffe place also had been fun. He'd never realized how huge they were until he, on a sightseers' wooden walkway, was head to head with a male whose two-foot tongue, gravelly and wet, unexpectedly caressed first him, then his grandson astride his shoulders. He had the photo. The bird place, well, birds lost their interest for him after the first flutter, rather like many parts of life itself.

"No, thank you. I have visited those. I think I'd like..."

The man interrupted.

"Perhaps then something farther. Gikomba Village, very good carvings. The Ngong Hills, very beautiful views of here and the Great Rift Valley. Maybe Lake Magadi and the Olorgesailie Prehistory place, where the famous Leakeys worked, quite extraordinary. We could arrange such. It is still early enough."

"No, thank you. They do sound nice, but today I'd just like to go out to the National Park. Is that possible?"

The man glanced at his watch.

"Of course. Can you return in an hour? The car and driver is fifty dollars and the admission is twenty U.S. dollars, if you please."

"Of course." He counted out the greenbacks while the Luo wrote a receipt.

"So, return here in an hour and all will be ready. *Asante sana.*"

"You're welcome. Thank you. In an hour."

"Indeed, yes. You will enjoy the animals, I know."

His driver spoke little English, but enough to point out and translate the names of places and presumably of animals. By Kenyan standards, he passed muster. They'd jolted out from Biashara Street onto Moi and pelted through the various belching and purring conveyances turning onto Haile Selassie Avenue and then Uhuru Highway with such force that his meal of Tusker and impala steak, taken not far from Biashara at the African Heritage Restaurant, rose in a nauseating glob. *Uhuru*, he remembered, had been the rallying cry—"Freedom!"—of Jomo Kenyatta's Mau Mau in the early '50s and of a potboiler by Robert Ruark. His driver, a Kikuyu whose Christian name was Matthew, turned at every pothole bump to flash a grin to assure him he wouldn't bounce out of the open Land Rover. Did he wonder why this older American wanted the National Park in the afternoon when few animals were in the open, and why did he wear that big knife? The grin didn't say, and he couldn't worry about Matthew's mental processes right now when he was trying to keep the impala down amid the stink of diesel exhaust and putrid garbage by the highway side where children played and goats foraged. From Wilson Airport, De Havilland Otters roared over them ferrying tourists to the Masai Mara and Tsavo where the elephants roamed and to Aberdares, Amboseli, Meru, Mount Kenya, Shaba, all the great parks where one might see animals and imagine the land as it once had been, as it had appeared to Finch-Hatton from his wire and fabric crate. Although even then, the great ground showed the tracks of vehicles bearing tourists and hunter-guides who bagged the rich men's trophies and, not infrequently, their wives. A final turn hurled him leftwards into Matthew, who seemed not to notice.

"To Main Gate now," Matthew said.

That was in the "now" of East Africa, meaning fifteen minutes of passing defunct strip malls, third world tire factories, car dealerships, a sports stadium, and sundry *dukas.* The main gate's guardians, dressed in paramilitary style, took the entry fee before beginning a long chat with Matthew. One handed him a brochure describing the park: 117 square kilometers; the oldest in Kenya yet still home to eighty animal species; possible place to view rhinos because the proximity to the city shied off poachers; perhaps 500 bird species; watered by Mbagathi River; adjoined by Animal Orphanage where offspring of dead animals (parents killed by predators, etc.) were raised. He'd nearly finished the brochure when the Land Rover bounded forward. Inside the guardhouse he could see assault rifles stacked. Waiting for fubar, snafu, somebody's fault.

Matthew took the route described in the brochure. To the main dam behind which the pitiful Mbagathi built up to be released periodically in dry times, and then onto the dirt track that led through "Lion Valley." The first animal, though, wasn't *simba.* A large reticulated giraffe stared at them, interrupted at feeding in a rare copse of deciduous trees. "*Twiga,*" Matthew said, pausing the vehicle and pointing. A snap with the throwaway froze the moment but didn't catch the intent assessment in the creature's large brown eyes. They bumped along, caught as fast in the ruts as if on rails. The park, he soon saw, was crisscrossed with roads, and one way of spotting animals was to see where the vehicles congregated. Matthew took a north track to the park's east gate. They followed the eastward road, which paralleled the main highway from Nairobi to Mombasa. At 300 yards he could hear the heavy trucks huffing toward the sea.

"*Bwana! Tembo!*" He followed Matthew's skinny arm. There toward the park's interior stood a clump of elephants, maybe 150 yards from them. He took the binoculars Matthew handed him. The great beasts came into focus, three cows, two with calves, and off fifty yards or so, what must be a bull. The females were spraying each other and their offspring with dust. The bull pulled clumps of grass to stuff in his big mouth. His ears flapped like Dumbo's.

"The man, he very dangerous," Matthew said. "They always alone except when making babies. You know, we never have *tembo* until poachers drive some here and *wazungu* save them for the park."

He was glad to know white people had some good effects with wildlife after the decades of killing safaris, not least by Hemingway. He stared at the huge animals, so different here than in a zoo. One female raised her trunk, and the cows and calves moved away toward some shrubs and trees that marked a watercourse. The male remained feeding. He wanted a picture, but they were too far off. Matthew put the Rover in gear. They cut southward along a road that bordered what the brochure called the Embakasi Plain. Here the acacia trees stood solitary, their umbrella foliage offering some shade and, for the hardy, some fodder. Animals moved in the distance, and with the glasses he could see them clearly: many Thomson's gazelles, their white fannies flashing as they loped, and a few Burchell's zebras grazing close to the trees like a herd of prisoner ponies. The Rover's jolting made it difficult to focus, but then Matthew topped a rise and stopped.

"*Fisi*," he said, nodding at the near plain. There skulked two silverback jackals looking for carrion or field mice, anything edible. "They always go in twos," Matthew said, "man and woman. Always together."

"Very touching," he replied. But what, he thought, if they tired of each other or became angry. Would they tear at each other as humans figuratively did? One of the jackals turned to look at the vehicle, then went back to foraging. The other's head came up as a large, strutting bird emerged from a gully.

"Secretary bird," Matthew explained. "See the crest? Royal-like."

Indeed, the bird was impressive, and big enough to cause the jackals to sidle away. The bird kept coming. It crossed the road a few yards ahead, sauntering into some tall grass. Impressive, but no more than the ground hornbills they'd just seen or, for that matter, the guinea fowls that looked like vultures. Matthew put the car in motion. He did have a tour to conduct, after all. They rumbled along, startling more gazelles and causing a troop of olive baboons to hurl shouts at them. One betesticled upstart charged the Rover, barking and showing large teeth.

"Even lions go round them," Matthew said, pulling the Rover onto the plain and around the animals. "Very mean." They hesitated while he took a snapshot of a female, her baby clinging to her reddish back. Back on the road, they turned on a track signposted Athi Basin. Appropriately, the ruts led down a broad slope. He pointed, gesturing for Matthew to stop. A group of Masai giraffes stood feeding on an odd tree with sacks hanging from it.

"We call it 'sausage tree,'" Matthew explained. "And see, past them?" He put the glasses where Matthew pointed, but it took a moment to find the black rhino. The animal had his head down, gouging at the earth with his horn. Bundles of dirt and grass descended, to be hoofed to separate the grass, which the rhino then ate.

"Very rare, the *kifaru*," Matthew whispered. "Until the bad hunters they were never here. Now the orphanage saves some babies, and some others came across the plain into the park."

"Can we get closer?"

Matthew shrugged. They left the track to bounce along toward the rhino. Suddenly out of a swale bolted three large antelopes. They roared away, their rears showing white horseshoe markings. He blinked, stiffened at the unexpected commotion. Matthew stayed calm.

"Waterbuck," he said. "*Hakuna matata*. No danger. Good luck."

The rhino, now fifty yards away, raised his great head. The binoculars showed his far-set eyes blinking. His armored sides heaved. He began to paw. Matthew stopped.

"No close," he said.

The throwaway's viewfinder showed a decent picture that could be enlarged. He snapped the shutter. Galvanized, the rhino swiveled to move toward them in a slow lope like something out of *Mogambo*. Its eyes, bright and bloody, seemed fixed on him.

"We go now," Matthew cried. He held on while the Rover did a 360. The knife handle, prodding his side, felt reassuring, while he simultaneously thought how absurd that would be. Soon the rhino was far behind, panting. They reeled onto the track. Matthew rose to stand while steering.

"Look, they have found cheetah." Matthew said. "They" consisted of three Rovers and a minibus, circled on the plain a quarter-mile ahead. Matthew careened their car from rut-side to rut-side while steering with one hand, waving his hat with the other. Somehow he'd descried a fellow driver semaphoring toward a lone acacia tree. They rolled into the circle.

"See," Matthew said. "Beside the stump of tree, the *duma*." The binoculars' lenses had fogged with the humidity of late afternoon. He rubbed them with his handkerchief. The cheetah stood oblivious near the stump. Her swayed back mimicked the curve of the stump and the characteristic streak of black trailing from her eyes like mascara tear tracks stood out against the yellow cat-face. The eyes turned toward their Rover. He could not find them baleful. Instead they seemed plaintive, reminiscent of his wife's when she was in a peaceful mode. Leave me alone, they seemed to say, just leave me alone. Yet to leave someone alone meant just that, didn't it? For the cheetah, a rare sighting he knew, maybe the yellow eyes signaled only that she would like to be looking at something other than these cars, these tourists, the interruptions to her life that were, now, her life. For an instant, he imagined she stared right at him with red-streaked yellow eyes, and he felt that electric chill again. He lowered the binoculars, took off his hat to wipe his face with its long bill. Matthew beamed at him as if to say, a cheetah, *bwana*, and for only $70! The animal hunkered abruptly. The tall grass swayed, marking her departure. He remembered the eyes. Motors started. The other cars growled away, but Matthew stayed standing, his nose pointing as if scenting something.

"*Bwana*, see what she sees."

He raised the glasses. Hulking against a smallish stand of trees just beyond the cheetah's stump now stood something that looked small but he sensed was large. He turned the center knob to focus. The swept-back horns and prominent nose marked a buffalo, the most dangerous of animals if alone, as this one was, and provoked, as this one was not. Cheetahs, baboons, even the plain's swiftest runners, the hartebeests and wildebeests, stayed far away from buffalos, whose only enemies were lions hunting in a pride and humans hunting without pride.

"No good to go closer," Matthew said, sliding down into his seat. "This one called *moran*, like Masai warrior. Old and with bad temper." The Rover moved. He snapped a futile long-range shot of the buffalo before holding on as they rocked down a ravine that brought them to the end of the park and the hippo pools. Here they dismounted to see the pig-like animals bob from the impounded water, blow aureoles of dank fluid, and submerge only to emerge showing bumpy skulls and close-set eyes. Two males did a competitive mating fandango like Olympic synchronized swimmers while a female coyly floated, watching.

"Very mean," Matthew offered. "More dangerous than buffalo, than lion. They feed at dark out on the plain."

"Yes, I see." Not much different from humans, he thought, depending on the prey, but he saw no more danger there than from a good fighting bull. Matthew motioned toward the lowering sun.

"We'll start back now, *bwana*. There are more animals, however."

They saw lions as they coursed the southern road: a weathered male and two females, one of which had two cubs. The family lay in ankle-length grass, snoring, occasionally scratching. The late light lit them with the golden sheen of *National Geographic* photos, but their eyes were closed. He thought of the big cats they'd seen in the Serengeti.

"They, too, go at night," Matthew said. "The women kill most."

He snapped a picture. The Rover bounced on. Matthew pointed out more sights, several hyrax against a rock outcropping, two eland, an impala, a family of warthogs so ugly only their own kind could care for them. They passed the turn to the Masai gate, chasing a giraffe off the track and bypassing a herd of loitering Grant's gazelles. The last of the tour resembled the first of it: same animals, same waving at other vehicles, bound past the western gates toward the Main Gate and the highway to Nairobi, to Nelson's barrier, to his family. The sun blinded them pulling up to the exit. The paramilitaries waved them through into the traffic, heavy in the late afternoon rush. Matthew hesitated before entering the highway.

"Good, yes?" he said. "Now do you want Biashara or to your house? No extra charge."

The diesel-blowing trucks lumbered past while sedans darted in and out of traffic lanes. He felt a sudden urge for a drink. The lump in his jacket comforted him. Faithful vodka. Or fubar, snafu, fault? The sun flashed a dim cheetah-yellow at him, although it wouldn't be dark in this latitude for three hours yet.

"The animal orphanage? Where is that?"

"No far down the road. I think they are closed now."

"Yes, well, take me there anyway."

A dirt road led off the raucous asphalt motorway for 200 yards or so, passing a *matatu* notice at the highway's edge. He could, then, make it back to the city center and beyond if need be. The approaching sign read, *Nairobi Park Animal Sanctuary.* He saw human figures moving in the fenced area behind the shuttered "Welcome Tourists" outbuilding.

"Matthew, I believe I will visit this. Don't worry. I can get a jitney from here."

Matthew's broad face creased, but his eyes showed no alarm. If anything, they read that this mad American wished to stay and look at parentless animals, so what was it to him? Maybe all whites were somehow *jinga* in the head.

"Here. Thank you for a good tour." He pressed a ten-dollar bill into Matthew's pale-palmed hand. "Thank you."

"*Asante sana, bwana.* But I must tell the shop you have decided to stay. It is not on me, correct?"

"No, not on you. I will tell them if they ask."

"Thank you. But I will say if you are not back by darkness to the shop, we will call the house whose number you gave. Or you may use the telephone by the road to us."

"Yes. So, I'll look at the little animals now. "

"As you like, be of good evening," Matthew said, starting the Rover. The car pulled away carefully so as not to spin sand. Matthew waved at the curve, and he waved back before turning to the orphanage building's porch. The entrance he could see was padlocked, but from the compound behind he could hear native speech and the scrape of large bodies moving. He moved off the porch, down a narrow path to a garden gate. In the slanting late light he saw two Kenyans with buckets, sloshing food to baby rhinos. They chattered, laughed at the animals pushing for the food. One put down his bucket to water the wallow. One rhino calf jumped in and rolled. More laughter. He moved along the chain-link fence until he was parallel with the feeders. A noise at his feet startled him. What? A dik-dik, a tiny antelope about ten inches at the shoulder, and this one seemed smaller, an adolescent. He could have stepped the life out of it. Instead he waved his booted foot and the brownish midget disappeared under a bush. To see a dik-dik was deemed good luck, he'd read. He moved on along the fence. The chatter and laughter grew fainter. Inside the fence he could see some warthogs and what looked like a leopard cub stretched on the limb of a scrub tree. He reached a corner where the fence turned toward a farm gate that must be the egress from the orphanage into the park whenever a sick or orphaned animal could be released to fend for itself. He imagined the predators just outside that gate, waiting for the infirm and innocent. Male or female, and did it matter?

In front of him ran a simple three-strand barbed wire fence, adorned with a triangular yellow warning sign. No gate, so it stood, obviously, only to mark the official edge of the park. Any determined animal could come and go if it wanted. But like humans most stayed where there was food, water, shelter, mating, a kind of safety, no matter the fubar, snafu, fault.

Back in the orphanage enclosure he heard a fence close, the rattle of buckets, and saw the light behind the reception building blink on. The equatorial African sunset came over his shoulder, from Karen and Langata. Directly behind him now, he reckoned, was the great Athi Plain leading down to Magadi, shadowed by the Nguruman Escarpment, down the Great Rift into Tanzania and the Serengeti. If he listened intently, he could hear the trucks off to his front, across the park, grinding toward the Indian Ocean and Mombasa. He pulled the vodka bottle from his jacket pocket, took a gulp, then put himself across the barbed wire. He felt for his knife. The night sounds were beginning. He thought he heard the growl of a lioness, the scream of a leopard. He took another shot of vodka. The light now came silver over the trees, the grass, whatever he might see. Something moved a stone's throw away. He bent, straightened to toss a dirt clod in that direction. A baboon barked, and he barked back. He felt the electric shudder. He gulped again, wishing for a Tusker back. He trudged down into a swale, listening to the bird cries, the deeper-throated communiques of larger beasts. A *tembo* trumpeted. He slumped against the swale's embankment and finished the vodka. The evening sounds engulfed him, the insects colluding in a symphony. He recalled the spiderwebbed windows. The moon began its slow ascent over the Ngong Hills, coercing the last sunlight into a union. Their light graced the feathery leaves of an acacia tree a few yards away. He drew a deep, liberated breath. All was well. He would wait. Anything fubared, snafued, was not now his fault.

VI

7-10

We were pimply-faced white kids with bad habits, but we could roll. Our sponsor-shirts gave away the bad habits. In elaborate gold scroll they spelled out Winckelmann Drugs. The scores showed the rolling. The five of us averaged 1,020 pins a game, 5,100 pins a series, thirty beers a night, and five hard-ons every time we bowled at the big places, where the girls and some women showed up to watch the pro teams, the Falstaffs and Budweisers and Carlings, and we beat them a few times but the big thing was we were virgins and lying about it, so it all came up open frames in the sex department. Until Violet came along.

She was really Kevin's girl, which was only right since he was the captain, the anchor guy, our big number-five roller. I was number two, the hole where you put the guy who can make spares but never turkeys out. Bob bowled first because if he didn't his mum got overworked. George came third because he was solid, and John fourth because he was streaky. We looked like a Norman Mailer infantry squad: A Jew, a Limey, a Dago, a

Kraut, and a Mick. We'd have had a black guy if we'd known one and he could roll, but in our neighborhood the closest we came to Negroes was seeing one in nine-inch living black-and-white standing next to Eisenhower. So it was just us and the downers John Winckelmann stole from his dad's store and the beers and Violet when Kevin brought her around the first time. Violet wasn't pretty. Later, after a marriage or two, I knew enough to look back and call her slutty attractive. But then, she looked exotic, and we were all strut and swagger and attitude, because we thought we knew that beneath all that exoticism lay an initiation beyond picking up the 7-10 split.

We bowled at Nelson Burton's lanes that time. Burton's was where the Budweisers practiced. Anheuser-Busch even gave them practice shirts, red and white with a big Bud Beechwood Aged logo to go with their big arms and bellies. Bobby, George, John and me lounged around teenage skinny in wash-pants and loud-printed shirts, looking cool with cigarettes and taking turns going out to my ancient Chevy every ten minutes for a beer and watching out for Kevin so we could start practicing. Old Nelson Burton, who'd been PBA champion three times, kept eyeing us from behind the Masonite counter. Punk kids, he called us, but we stood fourth or fifth in the City league, behind one or the other of the beer teams, so we just kept lounging, every once in a while rolling a practice shot, trying to split so we could work on the spares. I'd just nailed the 5-7 when Kevin finally strolled in.

"This is Violet," he told us. "The guys."

We each mumbled something. I think I said "how do you do" because my mother had been an Anglophile before she ran off with a drug company detail guy and just sent checks and cards to my aunt who sort of looked after me when she wasn't fighting with my uncle or at the Catholic church praying for my soul. Then we started to bowl, and Kevin wasn't with us. Oh, he picked up a ball and laid it out there, three boards right of the second-to-right mark, and he slid good and shook hands with the pins, but the little wrist flip wasn't there and there was no pin action, and he finished with maybe 155. The tell couldn't be missed. The guys and I saw it. Every time he rolled, he'd turn around and preen for Violet, who'd flash a nice grin and smooth her poodle skirt and give that little sitting-down hip-wiggle that girls did then instead of saying they wanted to get to know you better. Bob, George, John and I looked at each other hard when Kevin's second game came in at 162. Even old Burton, up there sharpening the scoring markers, looked down. He liked Kevin, thought he might make a pro-am tournament one day, even if he was a punk kid. But not averaging 160.

"C'mon," Bobby said.

I kept the church key and beer in the trunk of the Chevy. In the burning-leaves end of October it was still cold enough to drink, although not as much as when George had nipped it from the locker at his dad's tavern. Really, I suppose we were Class D juvenile delinquents. We were smarter than that, though. We could have moved up to Class A. We read Faulkner and Hemingway and the two O'Connors, along with all the trash we could find like eight-page bibles with Minnie doing dirty with Mickey and the Amboy Dukes drinking and fucking their way through the urban jungles. Bobby loved *God's Little Acre* and Kevin claimed to have read "intercourse parts" in his uncle's copy of *Ulysses* and George said this guy named Kerouac would have made a great sixth man and taught us how to steal big. But we didn't risk anything large. The petit bourgeoisie never do. So, we picked up a few things at the fringes, like the pills and the beers Bobby and I held while we pondered Kevin and the chick.

"So," he said.

"So, I think she's ruining him."

Bobby nodded just like his father did at the deli when some goy said something remarkably stupid, like what was the difference between corned beef and pastrami.

"No shit. What I meant was, what do we do?"

I didn't know, but because I never admitted I didn't know something, I had to pretend I had an answer. It was a trait that nearly ruined me several times in later life, but who can know something like that when you're eighteen and mock-bad?

"We got to make Kevin dump her."

"Yeah. You figure that out. Quick. We got the city tournament coming up, right?'

Bobby jabbed me in the chest, something he'd seen Brando or maybe Montgomery Clift do in *The Young Lions*.

"Knock it off. I'll dream up something."

We bounced our bottles under old Burton's car and went in to see Kevin finishing up a lusty 159. Violet sat sucking on a Winckelmann, meaning a juiced-up Coke, grinning at him and clapping her hands every time he went to the line. John and George stood watching with expressions like someone had just told them they had the clap. When they saw us, they took off for their beers, jingling my keys, while Kevin escorted Violet up to the pool tables. Bobby and I rolled a game each, but our hearts weren't in it and we quit keeping score in the sixth frame. When John and George came back we decided to adjourn to the only bar we knew that would serve us, a joint called The Stein Club, where we drank our opponents' sponsoring beer and shot the shit about the tournament, and the team wouldn't let me pay because Bobby had told them I'd fix it. Kevin and Violet weren't there. They'd waved a quick screw-you-we're-doing-it goodbye at Burton's, then hopped the crosstown for the deep southside where Violet seemed to live.

I dropped the guys off early enough so they wouldn't get their asses fried by parents wondering how between-college and/ or apply-at-the-packing-plant new high school grads could afford to bowl and carouse all night. My aunt and uncle were asleep. The fumes of bourbon hung heavy. I went up to the orphan's bedroom, listened to the last two innings of the Cardinals game, thought about how horny I was, and got hard and did something about it, and then got mad at Kevin and Violet for being them, being together. I did a crossword, but couldn't concentrate for thinking about how to mess up Violet and Kevin and to hell with the tournament, and the night passed and then it was dawn and I saw what to do.

Now, forty years later, I still think about it. I still feel it. Or maybe I just wish I could still feel it, have it, like it was. Strange how things are and aren't, so clear and alive in your mind but gone and dead in fact. It's almost enough to make you think about God. But with the city tournament coming up, the Winckelmann team couldn't afford thinking about God, not with Kevin thinking about Violet and the rest of us contemplating Kevin thinking about Violet. No, I had to make my plan and throw 300 with it.

"You guys in or not?" I asked them a week before the tourney. We lounged in the back booth at the Stein Club, smoking Larks and Luckies, nursing beers we had to buy so we always got Griesedicke Brothers, for the fun of saying it to the bartender. Polite people, especially girls, asked for a "Brothers," but we liked saying "gimme a greasy dick."

Bobby nodded and pulled on the Lucky. "You don't see him here, do you? He's out shtupping the bitch."

George looked at John who looked at George and they both looked at me.

"It isn't right, but we got to do something," John said. I knew what the qualifier was. Italians always got chilly toes unless they were mobsters because of The Church. Here John was hedging his bet: do it because it needs to be done even if it's wrong, sort of like the Crusades.

George was more pragmatic, and besides, his father bought us our shirts and paid the tourney fees.

"We got to go easy, but yeah, let's do it," he said.

Bobby nodded like his deli dad and signaled for another round to Stu the Bartender, who always looked at us like he hoped the cops would burst in and take us away, except then he'd lose his license. I sucked on my Lark, thinking now I had to set it up and was it all worth it. I went to the telephone and made the call.

The next night at Burton's the tension lay thicker than tobacco smoke, at least for the Winckelmann bunch. We threw the balls, we smoked, we watched the door, and when Violet at last swung in, her breasts all perky in a cashmere sweater, we exhaled almost in unison.

"Jesus, will you look at that," George said, as if we hadn't.

"That'll take the curve out of your hook," Bobby observed, ironic as usual.

"You're ready?" John asked, a task-minded Kraut, as always.

"Yeah, " I said, feeling as if I were in but not in this play, one part of me recording the pin noise, the smoke, the bullshit from the bowlers, the other thinking what am I doing now, what am I doing?

Whatever else she was, Violet was friendly. When I waved, she came over to the lane, accepted a Lark, accepted when I told her Kevin was held up, had to help one of his brothers with his homework, which I thought was a great excuse, making Kev all sweet and loving, which he actually was and that was the trouble. Now, Violet's friendliness came naturally, Kevin had said. Her mother was rumored to be over-friendly with the guys at the 555, a saloon around the corner from the Winckelmann Drug Store and one that wouldn't serve us. Her dad had decamped long ago, and mom didn't make anything at the 555 so she had to work the counter at Price's candy store by the grade school. From the time she was thirteen, Violet, Kevin said, clerked at the dime store way to hell and gone across Kingshighway, not just to help out but to put bologna on the table. She'd learned, he said, everything the hard way and knew that while everything had its price, you had to negotiate it yourself, taking what comes when it came because there was always a tomorrow and the bill that went with it. Actually, I think his words were, "she's tough, but not so tough, you know, and she don't know which way to turn."

"Hi, Vi," I essayed.

"Hi, Tommy. How's the score?"

"Holding our own, " Bobby said and laughed at his pun. He'd been hitting the Chevy trunk pretty good, but we all had. This whole thing was nerve-making.

"Hey," I said. "Have some juice," and I winked so big at her that George nearly dropped his ball on the approach and John had to study the score pad to keep from giggling.

"Thanks," Violet said, taking the cup Bobby poured from the extra-special Winckelmann-special Coke bottle. She drank steady-eyed, I think knowing what was up, and either caring or not, because we didn't know what waters she was in and vice versa. That night Violet seemed quite beautiful, her brown eyes clear and guileless, and yes, sparkly, and her dark hair shiny, curled around her ears in small arcs that reminded me of water waves. For a moment then, I imagined Kevin beside her, that odd big and blocky Celtic remnant, all bluster and pride above a rocky selfness that would never give in, which is what made him such a perfect number-five bowler or a lover or a friend.

Violet watched us roll out the practice line, only occasionally watching the swinging glass doors for Kevin. After her third hit on the Winckelmann-special, she sagged a bit on the beat-up wooden bench. Old Nelson Burton, whose geeky son was rolling next to us—and who would win the PBA championship in 1978—scanned us like a traffic cop, not saying "I know what you punk kids are up to."

The trip to the Chevy took no time. John took one arm, George the other. I paid old Burton, and Bobby went out to watch for Kevin's bus. Violet didn't mind kissing us, and she didn't care that we rolled up her sweater. Tits, I later learned, are mostly immaterial to women except in high emotional states like wanted-sex, baby-feeding, and threats of cancer. She lolled in the backseat. John, whose pharmaceutical interests were at stake, made a few gynecological moves. George wanted to screw her, but like all us virgins had the old call-of-conscience and couldn't. I sat, excited even if it was my scheme, in the driver's seat, watching for Bobby. When he started jumping, pointing at the arriving bus, I went around, shoved George out, shouted for him to get in the front seat, got in and unzipped, and I must admit, got harder. Violet's legs were spread like the 7-10, but she didn't seem so much like meat as she did like a victim, the sort I later saw in Vietnam, in Bangladesh, in Rwanda, in any place I was ever in. I remember watching Kevin pelting toward the Chevy, following Bobby's gesticulations. I remember saying to Violet, "take this," and I remember my penis in her mouth, which worked listlessly up and down below her fine eyes long enough for Kevin to yank open the Chevy's back door and jerk me out by my collars and haul Violet out where he could slap her hard several times, enough times that Bobby and John had to throw him down and hold him. I remember Kevin crying, and then thinking I should be crying, too, but it was all in a good cause. I believe young Nelson Burton arrived just then, and soon after George led the elder Burton and a herd of bowlers out to us. I remember standing up and zipping up and I remember how Kevin couldn't look at anybody and turned to Violet and let out a cry. If ever I heard a banshee, that was it. In those days, the cops weren't called. Someone—I think young Nelson—took Violet home. I peeled the Chevy out to my aunt's, where I sipped bourbon out of my uncle's liquor cabinet while they fought about his job and the bitch my mother was. John called later to say Kevin had calmed down, he understood, she was a whore, and while he'd like to kill me, we were still friends. The next day we bowled as a team in practice. Everybody stayed cool, smoking and going to the Chevy.

"Kevin," I said, between the first and second games, "I'm sorry, man. Things just got out of control. "

"Ain't it the truth," he said. "I'm OK now."

He was. On Thursday the city tournament started. We rolled good, averaging about 550 each. On Saturday night Old Burton sent us free pop before the finals. That night Kevin got it together totally, throwing an 806 series. Bobby threw like he was on Masada. George and John rolled in fear, which meant good, and I filled in some marks. We finished second. The Falstaffs beat us by 20 pins, but we smoked the Budweisers by 12. Our pictures got in the paper, and we each had a little trophy. Kevin, the captain, kept the big second place hardware, and then as often happens with teams, we broke up, we got jobs, went our ways. John took over the drug store. George got the family tavern. Bobby went to Princeton and became a philosophy professor. I eventually joined the Foreign Service, a diplomat to the end.

Kevin, well, he went into the construction business and made a fortune. His company's name is all over St. Louis. He married Violet a year after the city tournament. They had six kids—three normal, one priest, one nun, one suicide. I was godfather to the suicide. Ten years ago the Big Breast-C carried off Violet. Kevin didn't reset her. He never bowls now, and I didn't until my third marriage broke up when I started up again, half-assed. I send Kevin my scores by e-mail and he knows they suck. "You always threw splits," he says. Too many splits, too few conversions, and I never could throw strikes like Kevin did.

Chipmunks

I grew up on the south side of Chicago where in my neighborhood we seldom killed anything. Yes, there'd be the odd deaths around: a Negro (as we called them) a few blocks away, usually knifed. The occasional Italian shot to death or disappeared. A Mick or two beaten to death. The visiting lady or gentleman who was found in the lake or in one of the rivers with all identification and jewelry missing. But that was newspaper stuff, and I was brought up to be a gentleman, above such things. My mother, who was also my piano teacher, refused to step on bugs. She waited until my father came home. My father, a large man, squashed them mightily and my mother cried, holding me to her breast. My father worked in the stockyards in his boyhood. He bashed large animals with an iron rod, or later, put a bullet in the creature's forehead. After he was promoted and we moved to Chicago he oversaw their rendering into bacon, briskets (and corned beef), and other "cured meats."

My mother saw the point of this. She loved to eat meat, and so did I when I was old enough to know the difference between soft stuff and the real stuff. But as I said, I was raised between glissandos and briskets. So, when I left the third-story apartment we lived in to go to the music conservatory, it was with totally *salade mixe* emotions.

My first crush there was killing. She hailed, as we once said, from Des Moines and was knock-dead beautiful. Also better at piano than I was, so in the course of time, we dated—she liked my imitation Art Tatum right-hand riffs when we loafed playing jazz. I liked and copied her eloquent readings of Marion McPartland, Mary Lou Williams, and Count Basie. In bed we were harmonious if not rhapsodic. To put it bluntly, she preferred the upper octaves and I preferred the lower. But what a song we made on occasion. So I married her.

I should mention her name. It's Travi, for *La Traviata*, an opera about a whore. Her father loved the Verdi music. He played it in her nursery. I should also mention my name, which is equally odd. It's Jeremiah, after the mountain man. My father loved the tales of the mountain men because they fought Indians, married Indians, and above all killed big wild beasts.

Travi and I had an idyllic early marriage, unmarred by death unless you count divorce.

"Jerry," she said one morning, " I haven't been but with three other men, but they were all better in the sack than you. I'm going now."

So began my career as a bachelor cocktail pianist and in time, a zookeeper. The cocktail pianist (sometimes wedding pianist) gig was often fun. I played at a place called Frosty's in St. Louis, next to the Fox Theater. Why St. Louis? Well, my father had died suddenly—literally busted a gut—and my mother decided to be in the same city with her sister, and post-Travi I figured, why not go there, too. I rented a cheap place in midtown and enjoyed the city, especially what we then could call Dago Hill, where I played Italian weddings ("Josefina Please No Lean'a on the Bell" was a big favorite) and of course, the Cardinals in old Sportsman's Park, where they still had the Knothole section for kids. I also kept an eye on my mother, who had a few students in her big apartment but whose boozing I knew could only lead to an ugly dead end. Playing what the drunks in Frosty's wanted eased the pain of that, and my own sour moods "Stardust," "It Had to Be You," "Long Ago and Far Away," "Smoke Gets in Your Eyes" and especially "Melancholy Baby." Mostly weepy stuff, because drunks weep a lot. Sure, I slipped in some jazz standards. I'd just sort of mastered Brubeck's block chord method, so I practiced that. And I aped Ahmad Jamal, Keith Jarrett, Erroll Garner, George Shearing, players like such. I winced as I played because I was so far off the mark and I'd never get nearer to it. But it was a living. What changed the living was, at first, an encounter with the actress June Lockhart and her curmudgeonly actor-father, Gene. They blew in from the Fox's alley stage door one night (and many times thereafter). The Fox's management had decided to establish a quasi-repertory company, rotating plays with a core of actors and fleshing the casts out with local and regional actors. The Lockharts were one such core, so they could do *A Midsummer Night's Dream* one week and *Major Barbara* the next, and so on for six weeks. Nothing daring, alternating light and semi-light with an occasional tragedy thrown in so June wouldn't ever be mistaken for Lassie's mother. Then the Lockharts would move on to a tour and their movie and TV stuff, making room for the next core, people like Jan Sterling and Tab Hunter, and so on, until it was the Lockharts' turn again.

So, this first night June and Gene come barreling into Frosty's in Victorian dress. They were having a Wilde time in the theater. Clint the Huge, our bartender, pulled out two mixed martinis and handed them over. Clearly he'd been briefed on their preferences and time restraint. Gene glanced over at me while I was noodling "Satin Doll."

"Hey, kid," he said, moving toward the piano bar. "Can you play something to inspire us?"

"Sure. Anything in mind." I hope he had something in mind, because I didn't.

"Something classical," purred June, who'd moved like fog to the piano.

"Sure," I said again, trying not to look at her. The guy on my right, the only one at the piano bar, looked goggle-eyed, but then he usually did. The half-dozen regulars showed no interest, being deep into their Anheuser-Busch products. The three couples in booths stared at one another, probably uttering lies and wondering if all this was worth it.   I ripped into "The Minute Waltz," playing as fast as I could, covering up the right-hand mistakes with the bass ripples.   When I finished, June drained her glass, then turned her bright green eyes on me.

"That was lovely. You're…"

"Jeremiah."

"Thank you, Jeremiah. We'll see you often, I think. Come on, Daddy, we're on in six minutes."

They exited like thespians, throwing open the side door. Before it closed, you could see them putting on their stage faces for the last act. The Lockharts were true to their work. They came in often, in street clothes for a Ben Hecht play, in Shakespearean finery for *The Taming of the Shrew.* June seemed to me to fit her roles like the proverbial glove. Gene blustered through, she said, with considerable charm and talent. Then one day June came in alone, just before the performance. She wore a costume she said was for *Lady Windermere's Fan.* Her perfume tickled my nose hairs. I was alone at the piano bar. Goggle Eyes hadn't showed yet, and the other regulars were only now drifting in.

"Jeremiah," she cooed. "I have a favor to ask of you."

"Of course."

"We're going on tour, and I need something attended to. Can you come by our hotel tomorrow afternoon?"

"Yes," I said, in the unconscious way that one does when under a spell

"Wonderful! We're at the Chase Park Plaza. Come around three."

"Yes," I managed. She waved when she reached the side door, then vanished in a diaphanous cloud. Now what? I played

"September Song" to retain my mood. After work, which in those days was about 1 A.M., I went home and tried to sleep. "But sleep won't come the whole night through," ran in my head. Usually, I slept soundly even though redolent of cigarette smoke. The drinks I had when we closed helped. But this night, I couldn't drift off. Visions of the Lockharts danced in my head, especially of June in her many roles, each lovely, each with its own costume and face. Her dress and makeup changed with each show, so that although I knew it was she, it was not; it was as though I had to look through something to the real person. Gene was different. No matter how dressed or made-up, big Gene appeared like a skeleton on an X-ray. I tossed and turned. When my mother called at 3:30 A.M., I felt relief. Talking with a drunken relative can be healing. You transform her problems into yours, thereby losing yours. This time it was her latest suitor. She felt like she was in *The Glass Menagerie*, she said.

"Break all the dishes," I told her, "and go to bed. We'll talk more tomorrow."

When tomorrow came I awoke as if underwater. I killed most of the day napping and practicing. I even hit the Hanon to sharpen my technique in case another classical request came from the players. Running those rote exercises, a shopworn epiphany visited me. It went: all men are vulnerable to women from birth to death, and all men transcend to helplessness when confronted with pretty women. Thus armed I set off for the venerable Chase Park Plaza Hotel.

This, obviously, was some time ago. Hotels were grand but still to human scale. This one had a large marbled lobby, damask drapes, the usual oversized potted plants, a discreet area off to one side where a piano lurked and the ghosts of patrons of cocktail pianists waved from the little tables. At the end of the lobby sat an imposing oak reception desk with the usual clerk smirking under the Art Deco chandeliers and fluted sconces.

"May I help you," he asked. From my jaundiced view as a professional observer—I spent a lot of time watching people while tinkling my chords—I judged him to be my age, pushing thirty, like me not quite past some minor shaving challenges, but unlike me without a clue as to how the world works. If playing cocktail piano teaches you anything, it's that humans are sequentially the most divine and disgusting mammals on the planet. You have to watch for the shift in their winds, as I did when learning to sail in my Camp Lincoln days. This guy looked like he couldn't distinguish a breeze from a gale.

"Yes, could you please connect me to Miss June Lockhart's suite?"

"Miss Lockhart? She doesn't usually let fans visit."

"She's expecting me. I'm not a fan. I'm her pianist."

"Oh, OK. House phone's there." He waved a spindly arm toward a side counter.

"Thank you."

"Sure. She's a nice lady."

"Yes."

The phone's ringing unnerved me. What if all this was a fantasy, me and a hotel and June Lockhart? But she picked up the receiver on the third ring.

"Miss Lockhart?"

"Yes, Jerry. You don't mind if I call you that."

"No, no, not at all."

"Well, come on up. We're in the penthouse on nine. You can't miss it."

The elevator smelled, as they once said, swank. A hint of lilac, some furniture polish wafting from the oak panels. I'd almost expected a man with a brass control wheel to take us from floor to floor, but there were Bakelite buttons. I pushed the top one. The car ascended with appropriate dignity. I thought of Gershwin and Levant, Rogers and Astaire, Burns and Allen, and for some reason Jung and Freud. I felt a long way from Chicago's streets, from my mother's pretensions (although they'd stood me in good stead), from Frosty's, from schooling, most of all from the self I thought I was.

The elevator sighed to a stop, and I stepped onto the Oriental-patterned carpet. Directly in front of me a double oak door guarded the Lockharts. I flopped the brass knocker against the fragrant wood. In a minute, I heard footsteps. The door swung inward, and there she was, radiant in a kind of afternoon dressing gown if there is such a thing. Silk, it looked like, in lavender and soft green, quite clingy. She wore the lightest of makeup, doubtless because that evening she'd have on her thick Fox Theater face.

"Come in, please, Jerry."

I followed like Lassie into the suite. We moved past a baby grand piano toward a settee, or sofa-thing that overlooked Forest Park and the buildings receding westward across Kingshighway and down Lindell Blvd where stately homes housed the glitterati. I could barely make out some of the St. Louis Zoo buildings southward in the park. Now, I realize they held more than a view.

"Jerry," she said, after we were seated. "Would you like some coffee, or tea? It's just a phone call away."

"No, thanks." If I took anything, it would be a stiff drink, and I was afraid I'd spill that.

"Well, then, to my favor."

She leaned back abruptly as if to distance herself from the favor-doer, as if a scrim had lowered between us. I was just the piano player now, come to call, and yet, I would then somehow realize that conviction that all men are vulnerable to women, especially mothers and pretty women.

"This is rather delicate," she said. "That's why I asked you to come by while Gene is napping."

"I understand," I said, although I wondered at the mewling sounds coming from behind the northern doors that I assumed led into a bedroom.

"Well, the fact is that I want you to kill my dog."

I can't recall how my face and body reacted then. I have an image of myself, cool and collected, nodding after she uttered her favor. But I'm sure that's wrong. More than likely my jaw dropped, my eyes glazed and I nodded like a steer in the killing chute. But I know I spoke.

"Kill your dog? You want me to kill your dog." Lassie's mother wanted me to kill her dog.

"Yes, please. There's a hundred-dollar fee, naturally."

I recall she sounded remarkably like Travi then, the time I was told about how I'd been cuckolded and was persona non grata. June Lockhart, though, wasn't icy. Just resolved, like she was reading lines.

Much of the rest of the interview has blurred, except for the distinct memory of wanting that stiff drink, and maybe tinkling off a few tunes on the baby grand. So much for dreams of an affair to remember. She went to the northern bedroom doors, I remember, opened them, went inside, and emerged with a small scabrous canine in her arms.

"This is your charge," she declaimed. "Gene can't abide poor Portia any longer, nor can I. She's suffering so. Here, let me wrap her." From the north bedroom she came with a Chase Park Plaza bathrobe, soon wrapped around Portia "There, there, darling," June Lockhart murmured. She now was the actress, not the enticing, charming, rather normal person for whom I'd played the piano.

"Please, Jerry."

I guess I stood up to receive Portia and the Ben Franklin stuffed into my rear pocket. The touch of her hand on my bottom almost rekindled something, but the dead-flesh odor of Portia overwhelmed Dr. Freud. The next thing I remember about the hotel interview was scurrying through the lobby with the clerk's farewell in my ears.

"Got her another butt-boy, huh? That dog gonna walk you, ha ha?"

I suppose she'd pecked me on the cheek when I left. I imagine Old Gene guffawing behind his south bedroom doors, and perhaps June and Gene celebrating like the Macbeths after

Duncan is murdered. Whichever, it all had a Shakespearean tinge to it. But Portia? A different role, and there was no quality of mercy in my mission.

Travi visited my workplace at the St. Louis Zoo yesterday. She'd broken up with number thirty-eight or whatever he was in her platoon of admirers. She was in St. Louis for a music conference and inquired of me at my mother's. She asked how I was, if I regretted playing the piano only for myself, if there was a chance for us to reconcile. Chipmunks scampered out of the low stone wall where we sat outside the cages that held the dingoes, hyenas, and wolves. Travi fed the chipmunks peanuts bought out of a vending machine. The wild dogs weren't impressed. Their keeper had already thrown them their meat and bones. Travi was not interested in the dog family. After she left, sobbing that we'd had so much together, I hummed "The Minute Waltz." I'd played it a last time for the Lockharts the night their show closed, one night after I'd been vouchsafed Portia. They were replaced by some touring thing called "Lullaby of Broadway." June hugged and kissed my cheek, asking whether I'd taken care of Portia. I nodded and played "Somewhere Over the Rainbow."

No lie, either. The evening after my visit to the suite, I took Portia to the closed zoo. It wasn't difficult to sneak past the old rear gate. I stood with this smelly old toy poodle in my arms, again wrapped in the fancy hotel bathrobe. Animal noises floated in the summer twilight: birdcalls, snuffling and shufflings, brays, an elephant's trumpeting. A few stars shown, and a sliver of a moon, but mostly the illumination came from the city lights, the museum's and the zoo's floods. Portia sighed and farted, barely breathing. I could have taken her to a vet, but I was sure June and Gene had often done that. Therefore, for the great Lockharts, I was the easiest way out for them. I was the poodle-patsy. I thought how nice it must be if you were like Travi flitting from lover to lover hoping one would stick before you aged too much, or like the Lockharts, portraying prominent characters without having to know anything but the lines.

That night I approached the wild dogs' cages. It would have been an easy toss. Portia weighed less than a basketball. When I raised her to toss-level, she gave out a whimper, a G-major. I lowered her and sat on the stone wall. Portia cast an opaque eye at me and blinked. What had the poet Richard Wilbur said, something like, "beasts in their major freedom?" I figured that included humans, too, whatever form that freedom took. I tucked Portia under my arm for the walk back to my old Chevy. She didn't have long. What the hell, just a different riff. I will make her comfortable. I will let her die as she wills. I will give her a decent burial in her robe. I will take a photo of her gravesite and send it to the publicist for the Lockharts, along with a corny song lyric, "I can't stop loving you." I will sign it, "Portia."

We made it safely out of the gate. A chipmunk darted from the foliage into the glare of the parking floods, maybe thinking it had suddenly become dawn. He stopped as ground squirrels will to take a peek at us. Portia almost raised her head.

She died two days later, and I did the burial and the photo. Then I applied for a job at the zoo. These days I play piano for myself during the night. I don't drink since my mother died of the stuff. I've never heard again from the Lockharts. During the day I feed my wild dogs and at night the corps of nocturnal chipmunks, who are more grateful.

The Novice Writer Explores
Cartography

A ping Yeats, I've sought my theme in vain. Too many times. Yet the story urges itself. It isn't a question of elements. I have those. There is a boy whose sweat rancors the funeral-chapel limousine on both occasions. There is the town both times, a Norman Rockwell town, with wide streets and open faces on the passersby. There is both times the cemetery, surrounded by cornfields, a small green square set in the gold. Other elements, too. Flowers. Relatives. Weather.

What's missing is the theme. It can't be simply death. Nor maturation. Nor any other off-the-shelf catchall. It is, I guess, something like the coordinates of grief. But how to render that? How explain just what it is that this boy becoming man felt.

It is his father in the long metal box. His father dead from a hole somewhere in his intestines. His father for whom he prayed and whom he believed was stronger than the strongest sickness.

His father who taught him how to bunt, to read books, to cry only when it hurt too much. They lower the metal box. The straps creak. The wind blows. The corn's leaves and husks rub. The corn makes the sound kids make when they put a leaf between their thumbs and hiss through it. The metal box is down. A stranger says the prayers. His mother, whom he should hold, is hugged by her mother. He stands to the side, awkward, feeling that he is not here, that the wind will blow all this away like it blew the heat shimmers from the metal box. No townspeople are there. His father left this place long ago. Only his name, the name of his father's father and of what will be the boy's children persists, etched into the granite brought from the Rockies by the Union Pacific.

Is that grief? Rendered grief? By art's standards it is only an emotional moment in the psyche. Dragged out this way its sentimentalism shows. That, of course, one day might be the armature of something sturdy, but today it is only a stark, one-dimensional wire. So, return to metaphor. Meridians of grief, I suggested. Meridians are lines of cartography. They form great circles around the earth, passing through the poles. They show location. The meridian of Greenwich also determines time. Meridians are where and when.

Another time. Another metal box. His mother is inside. The heat waves rise again. A different stranger drones on about being unafraid in the valley of death. The boy is not afraid. He is tired and angry. He has come with the box on the Union Pacific, sitting up all night and day, watching for the hills to flatten and the corn to begin. The men at the depot touched the box gingerly, respectfully, as though it contained a powerful medicine. But it held only remains. The tissues are full of alcohol and barbiturates, but they are only remains. His mother's mother cries again that the boy's mother was not that kind of woman. The wind again clacks the corn. Again he feels awkward, but mostly angry. His mother's husband, not his father, is here. He's drunk and sobs in stagey grief. The granite will bear his name...

So. There the boy is set in another location and in an idea of time. But what the boy felt, apparently, is nothing. And all the grief, the theme, is retrospective. That raises an interesting question: If the boy felt nothing then, how can I make him feel something now? That's not a question for art, of course, which is concerned with effect, not process. Maybe the answer is that he doesn't need to feel anything now, but only needs to seem as if he had felt something. Is texture all?

In the hospital the doctors said his father was getting well. Antibiotics were wonderful. The hole in his guts had poisoned him, but the drugs would fix that. They were so sure that they let the boy visit. Let him watch his father pick at the covers with long, fielder's-glove fingers. Let him hear his father shout, "Goddam it! Get out of the flowers, you're squashing the blossoms, Goddam it!" His father had lucid moments, too. He asked the boy how school was going, how the White Sox were doing, and if he was helping his mother. The doctors were so sure they told the boy's mother to let him go out on Friday night, and when he came home from the movie his mother's mother folded him into her big arms and told him. Then she cried, and he felt that somehow it was all his fault. That if he had not gone out, not booted a ground ball, not been at all, he would not then be falling fast through darkness.

This then, you see, is as recorded now. To try for more precise texture—how strong the grandmother's arms were, what scent she wore, how late they stayed up, how the funeral plans were made, how much the adults drank—could be interesting. But art has to be edited, compressed, doesn't it, so the theme stands clear? Some things have to go. Like the fact that these characters undoubtedly would have recalled the father's joke that he was so poor he'd have a one-car funeral. Surely, too, the mother would have wept and told the boy he'd have to be the man now. He would agree, of course, and have no idea what she meant. But let those go. Pursue the theme, the prevailing emotional valences. Who and why and how the weather was…

When the front and rear doors of the apartment were open, the icy wind poured in like water. "The Hawk" they call that wind in Chicago. Leaving, the coroner had left the front door open. The rear door was open because the boy's stepfather had stumbled out that way to call the police when he'd awakened and found dead beside him, spittle drooling from her mouth, the boy's naked mother. Neighbors stole appliances and gadgets while he was gone. The policeman said the stepfather had to mumble his message several times because he was too drunk to talk straight. Her pubic hair was blonde. It was gummy, the coroner reported. Her heart had stopped, the coroner said, because of bourbon and phenobarbital. She was at the mortician's when the boy arrived. He chose her metal box, as gold as he could get. He brought with him her burial clothes. A white linen dress and black-bead jewelry. Her gold-blond hair he had swept back in soft curls. He insisted she wear shoes. When he returned to the apartment the rear door was still open. The stepfather sat in his father's red leather chair, drinking vodka. He smelled because he had beshit himself. The boy did not let the stepfather sit beside him on the train taking the box west. When he cried he did it alone. He thought over and over about how six hours before she died she had called and said, "Come get me! I've had enough." Not long after the funeral the boy married.

Now does that go far enough? Grief's coordinates, like Rand McNally's, intersect at many places. I suppose those junctions constitute theme. The trouble is, there are so many intersections. They form a vast grid of feelings, and so when you approach a junction you can feel all along it, in all directions, like putting your hand on a harp and plucking just one string.

Infinite harmonic vibrations. Seeking the theme is seeking the intersection of the main emotions.

The last time the weather was cold. The corn was stubble. Frost held on the cemetery's stiff brown grass. The grass crunched when the boy walked on it. He recalled Whitman: the uncut hair of graves. At the first grave he ran his fingers over his name, cut deep against the harsh climate. He put a red mum in the bronze-painted urn. Then he walked to the second grave. He did not look at the name that was not his. He tried to stare through the earth but saw only the stiff brown grass. He put a white mum in the urn. He walked a hundred feet, turned and looked back. He sighted along the line between himself and the two graves. If continued, it would go around the world, then curve into space as part of the celestial sphere, of the great circle. It would pass through everyone standing on its path before coming back through him and the graves. It was, he saw, a meridian, and its compass point would never change. He stood for several minutes, feeling its intersections. Then he drove home over a different line to his wife and children.

You see how vexing this theme seeking is? Do I have it? Or have I only come at another time in vain? Art is tricky. Grids, intersections, junctions, meridians of grief all only approximate what I felt. Perhaps approximations is the theme. Still, one must keep seeking. I can always start again in Yeats' foul rag-and-bone shop of the heart. I can always repeat to myself the fundamental elements: that I still weep because I miss them and because I could not save them and because I cannot say so well enough.

Memorial Day

D riving into town, he had a familiar, unwelcome sensation: a tingling that always told him he ought to be having some deep emotion, but he wasn't, and so he would, later, be guilty about that. Sort of an early warning system that he hadn't wanted installed. To stop the tingling he turned to the fields stretching away westward beneath the heat shimmers. Corn, mostly, and milo. Some oats. Waving fields that beckoned travelers farther and farther out until the water became scarce, the fields dried to rough pasture, the mountains rose to mark one part of the world from another. A blast of air conditioning tickled his nostril hairs, and he was glad he'd never live in this country.

"This is it," he said to her.

"It's like I imagined it," she said. "Has it changed much?" Her short gray-brown hair jiggled now as they hit the cobblestones of the main street.

"I don't know yet," he said. "I haven't been here for fifteen years, and I was just passing through. Before that, thirty, at my mother's funeral. Forty since my father's."

She smiled. "Why," she said, "that goes back even before you and me."

He watched her eyes scan the block's storefronts: the Big Red Café, a ladies-wear store, a Rexall, the Sears outlet, oh, yes, Sears, the REA office, a Farmers Savings branch. Like him, when she held her face down to peer over her glasses, the nascent double chin showed. How strange, he thought, to be irrevocably middle-aged and yet so often feel young, so often feel dumb and vulnerable. He was lucky in one way, she'd said. His hair, graying from its blond, still looked golden in certain lights.

"I'm going to ask at that café," he said. He pulled the Chrysler into the curb at an angle.

"Look," she said. "No meters."

"Of course not. Nebraska is God's country. Ask anyone in it. They probably don't even charge interest on loans."

She laughed and looked girlish again. He stepped into the afternoon heat. The air smelled like popcorn, and he remembered that there was a co-op elevator and processor somewhere in town. He ducked under the café's awning, pulled, then pushed the door to come into the aromas of coffee and fried foods. The waitress gave him a big grin when he asked directions.

"Which cemetery you want," she said. "Catholic or other?"

"Other," he said. Lord, these native Lutherans didn't even want to be buried next to a Papist. His mother had felt the same, and she'd even been raised Catholic, though with an apostate nature.

"Go down to Sixth Street," the woman was saying. "Turn west and go until you come to Barker's Nursery. Turn north and look west. You'll see the cemetery. Just drive right on in. Can I get you some coffee or anything?"

"No, thank you. I appreciate the information." She smiled again. "I'm visiting my parents' graves," he said, and immediately wondered why on earth he'd told her that. The woman nodded, still smiling.

"Thanks again," he said.

He found the LeBaron running. She sat with all the vents turned toward her.

"God, it's hot," she said. "Did you find out?"

"Yes. Do you want to go there now, or should we find a motel and go in the morning? It's pushing five. How about some nice A/C, a few drinks, a swim, and maybe a bit of carnal knowledge?"

Her wide brown eyes inventoried him. A thing he loved in her was the swift, almost always right instinct.

"Is that what you want? I think you really want to go and look, but you're afraid it'll spoil the day."

"It wouldn't spoil the day," he replied, but he felt himself lying. The trip was a self-imposed duty, he knew, born out of a childhood training that had burned into him the obligation to somehow, someday, honor his father and his mother, and all that was fine, but he'd been supposed to do that while they were alive and he hadn't, and this sentimental journey couldn't redeem that past, but what the hell, he had to do something or his old friend would always be with him, dressed in his parents' graveyard clothes, although guilt had a closet full of other garments, and why did he walk hand-in-hand with guilt anyway? Why not just clasp guilt's lesser friend, sorrow, in honor of those people so alive in his memory but so dead just down Sixth Street to the west?

"It wouldn't spoil the day," he repeated. "But I'm whipped. Let's find a place to stay."

There wasn't much to choose from in Glencoe. A Super 8 and a Comfort Inn near the interstate, both crowded with eighteen-wheelers and RVs. Closest to town was a Best Western, huddled like a preschool Lego building on the west side of the old highway. A south wind chopped the surface of the swimming pool, hardly bigger than his. That wind chilled, too, after he emerged, chlorined, to stand wondering how many times his father had peered out from his hometown at this lowering west sky, the amber-gold going to an amethyst-purple smudge laying like a black snake across the horizon. Hell, the wind stirred his drink. How did people live here?

"What do you suppose my father felt looking at this," he asked her, "day after living day?"

"Didn't he ever say?"

"He never talked about his feelings. I only remember him saying he couldn't wait to leave town."

"And went all the way to Omaha." She pushed her sunglasses up so she could stare at the setting sun.

"Yes. Omaha."

He felt nettled, unreasonably. He held no brief for Glencoe. Or Omaha. He'd spent, or squandered, his life in larger cities around the world. No reason to feel allegiance to this place. Or any other. Not his ground, no more to him, logically, than to the two kids splashing in the shallow end, or to their parents, wide-hipped and road-weary, keeping one eye on their children and the other on their packed car. Minnesota plates, he noticed, and a GO VIKES! bumper sticker.

"When did he leave," he heard her ask through the gale.

"He went to the University. Then law school. Then Omaha. He wasn't here except for visits, I don't think, after he was eighteen."

She rose from the plastic-latticed lounger to drape a motel towel around her freckled shoulders.

"Well, he's here now to stay. I'm going in. I feel like I'm being blow-dried."

He watched her pick her way barefoot across the hot asphalt, lifting each foot like a show horse. He remembered that: the burnt rubber smell, the sole of your foot or shoe tentacled to it like a piece of pizza lifted from a pan. Remembered it in New York, Cairo, Singapore, Perth. And so? What good was such a memory? Shouldn't memories be specific, linked to a single place, so that whatever was recalled unsheathed a sword-slash of time past? People who'd stayed put in Glencoe probably had those kinds of memories. He had mental postcards.

He threw back the diluted vodka and tonic. The little Minnesota boy rushed past him to jump in the pool, his mother's eyes checking him over the edge of her Coors Light. The boy, dark against the sunset, froze for a millisecond at the height of his jump. The plummet threw water on the concrete skirt, where it sizzled, then evaporated in a skirl of vapor. Boys, water. But in his father's time it was probably a swimming hole on the creek, Beaver Creek, the sign said, that threaded the town on its way to the Platte. The Platte river, center line for the Oregon trail, the proverbial stream too thick to drink, to thin to plow. But OK for wet. He arced the plastic drink cup into the trash barrel.

The room's darkness hurt his eyes. He blinked, found the switch for one over-bed light. She lay curled on her side, dozing. He settled on the edge of the other queen size. How innocent sleeping people always looked, as if just created, no matter what their age. In sleep she looked young again, as when he'd first met her. The lines soft, the tight, anxious look gone. He closed his eyes, trying to force pictures of his children when they were little, asleep with stuffed animals and books and baseball gloves, or cuddling one of the long-dead cats or dogs, and the pictures came, fleeting as eye blinks, in a succession of ages until he saw his daughter and son asleep with their lovers, safe in late-afternoon naps in faraway cities in other countries. He tried to imagine himself as little and asleep, too, with his father watching him, tried to see his father napping in this town, but he couldn't get either image because he could never see himself or know his father. Maybe to see such things you had to be as innocent as sleepers looked. He stood, moved to the vanity's sinkboard, and mixed another drink. The rattle of the ice disturbed her.

"Hi," she murmured. "I guess the sun got to me." She stretched, bowing her back so that her breasts thrust hard against the bathing suit. Like his mother, she was small boned but well proportioned. He must have been three or four when first he'd noticed his mother's breasts, not in any sexual way, but as a curious feature of her anatomy unrelated to any suckling he might have done. It wasn't until much, much later that he ever tried to imagine his parents making love, so much later it was after his first masturbations, after Joyce Whatever-her-name-was had kissed and touched him. Seventh grade? After his father died and his mother remarried, he violently repressed any thoughts of her sexuality. The thought of her writhing beneath the loathsome new husband who'd bought her as surely as any whore brought his gag reflex into full operation, even now. He drained the vodka and tonic.

"Do you want another?" he asked her.

"Please."

He mixed it and carried it to her. Always been good at fetching and carrying. His forte with his mother, during her widowhood, although she made bartending easy, taking her vodka straight except for a dash of bitters.

"Thanks. You look cute in your suit," she said.

"Cute?"

"Sort of grown-up sexy."

"Sort of?"

"Not bad for a middle-aged guy with strong hormones and most of his hair." She put her hand on his genitals. "And only a few extra pounds in the love handles."

"You can't drive a spike with a tack hammer," he said, taking his drinkless hand inside the Lycra to her breast. She shuddered, slapped her drink on the table, and then their four hands were all free and they were out of the suits, on the big bed and into a lovemaking that seemed to take a long time. They began with her astride him, until he bucked her below him like a good missionary, but they finished in Russian style, she prone, uttering the small cries he always associated with injured animals, and he, his belly bumping buttocks, trying to dam both his orgasm and the unbidden images, for lovemaking should be focused, he professed, and singular, not clotted by the true past or imagined future. But the dam, as always, burst, and he finished while she cried out his name and that of God. Then they lay in the sweat-sheen holding each other in the awkward way of humans returning from the joyous animal to the regretful rational.

"You're wonderful," she said.

"We're wonderful," he corrected without thinking. This dialogue they'd often had.

"Whatever."

They lay listening to the air conditioner throb until it was full dark outside and she disentangled to shower. He made them more drinks. While he bathed, she made more, too. And so they were giddy setting out to find a restaurant. The motel guide proved that a town of 7,000 didn't offer much. He'd settled on a place with the biggest ad, The Last Chance, between Fifth and Sixth streets. a block west of Main. They bumped along the cobbles, made the turn, and came into a large parking lot packed with cars set midway between The Last Chance and the American Legion club.

"One or the other has good food or whores," she said.

"Let's take The Chance," he said.

They found it flossy. Plains Victorian, he could call it. Stained glass, brass fittings, cherry tables, carved wood bar. No Muzak, just the flutings of what must have been 5 percent of Glencoe's population. He put his name on the dining list, and they waited in the bar. He watched her eyes study the people, moving from one to another as though seeking identities. To him they all looked Midwestern Gothic. Women in discount-store dresses or slacks and low-end designer blouses. Men in sport shirts and Sansabelt trousers. Both sexes big and talkative, not afraid to show they ate well or had opinions. A few older men preened in yellow Lions Club tunics festooned with service patches. Yet the crowd looked, he thought, somehow wholesome, as though they'd assembled out of duty.

"Conaway," came the call.

"Age before beauty," he said, sweeping his arm toward the dining room.

"Pearls before swine," she retorted, and they laughed moving into the Last Chance's salon. How sophisticated it was to use the Dotty Parker-Claire Booth Luce repartee. And how irrelevant here. Actually, the Last Chance's extensive menu was pretty sophisticated. He doubted his father had ever had presented in Glencoe choices like braised quail or lemon-pepper sole. No, he bet it'd been sirloin or chicken-fried steak at the Big Red Café, over next to Sears.

"So, what will you have?" he asked after their wine arrived.

"Fettucine Alfredo," she said.

"Fettucine? Are you kidding? This is Nebraska, not Italy. You eat meat here. Steaks. Chops. Poultry. Rare beef, cooked pig, breaded chicken. All of them with potatoes and butter and gravy, two vegetables, a salad and, for dessert, apple pie or crumble with vanilla ice cream. Got it?"

"Fettucine Alfredo."

He waved over their well-fed waitress, and with a mock scowl, ordered her noodles and a steak for himself.

"What time do you want to go tomorrow?" she asked.

"I don't know. In the morning. I need to buy flowers."

"You'll feel better afterwards, won't you?"

"I hope so," he said, watching her eyes flick to the nearest stained glass. Nerves or avoidance? "Well, different kind of crowd in there, eh?" he said. She took the gambit and they discussed the place and people until the food came.

Miraculously, he thought, her fettucine was perfect. But his steak, ah, that showed Nebraska at its best. The meat had been hung, aged, then broiled just right, so that he could almost feel the animal's strength coming into him. They had brandy with the coffee, and she displayed what she called her Italian Midwesterner balance by taking on the apple pie and ice cream. The bill came to $24.79. In Tokyo, it would have been $247.90.

"Care for a waddle?" He floated the words into the warm, wet evening air to compete with the music billowing from the Legion club. The sad country songs pinged off the parked cars like sonar.

"Sure. I'll work off the pie." They started toward the club.

She hooked her arm around his. "Was Charley Starkweather from around here?" she asked.

"Why, you feeling murderous?"

"No, but was he?"

"Farther west. But he killed some folks on a farm between here and North Platte. He and his girlfriend, what was her name?"

"Carol Fugate. She's out now. Rehabilitated they say."

He sang, "Some people say there's a woman to blame."

"Satan is male," she said.

"Just a big old phallic snake. No wonder Eve couldn't say no."

She moaned, the sound nearly lost in the music as they passed the club entrance.

"Why, why, oh God, isn't there another sex. Where are we going?"

"Just here, out to Main," he said, "then down Eighth."

The street gleamed beneath the lights as empty as if a neutron bomb had radiated all the citizens and left the buildings standing. A few signs glowed. Sears, Rexall, Big Red Café, but only the Budweiser sign in the Lincoln Bar and Grill signaled an open business. They walked on, heels clicking, passing the new library, then the Federal-style municipal auditorium. He wondered what they might do in there, sheltered from the big sky by the good old WPA workmanship. Built long after his father had left. Besides, his father had hated the New Deal. Took away individualism. But individualism hadn't gotten his father much, or his mother. They'd never owned a house. Didn't have a car all the time he was growing up. They weren't poor, but the American Dream Express never stopped at their door. Had it at his? What would they make of his career? At least he'd made money, not that he was rich, just comfortable enough to indulge himself and a few selected others.

"Stop!" she said. "Smell that!"

Like a whoaed team, they halted on the pitted sidewalk. Lined along the cobbled street stood frame houses, some of them substantial. Sweetgum and cottonwood trees bowered the street. He inhaled. What was it? The scent drove him back in time, tumbling through years, until he could fix it, could feel his skin prickle in emotional time travel. Sure! His grandfather's house, the home of his mother's father. His throat tightened.

"It's honeysuckle," he coughed.

"It's like liquid," she said, "it's all over me like jam. I swear, I feel sweetened."

"Pain in the ass if you let it go because it's hardy. Even grows in this terrible heat."

She tilted her face up to take in the odor. The streetlamp's glare deepened the crow's feet and laugh lines, but her smile smoothed them.

"I forgot," she said, " you know all those gardening things."

He strained toward the nearest house, looking for a number. "OK, just another block."

"What is?"

"The house where my father grew up, 424 East Eighth. It's in the family Bible."

In the evening quiet, their footsteps sounded ominous, but no porch lights clicked on in alarm. Televisions flickered in parlors, as these unafraid folk would call them. An occasional cough drifted from a bedroom, and air conditioners whined against the heat. In one upstairs window he saw a boy hunched over a book, his profile sharp in the gooseneck's light.

"Isn't that it?" she said, pointing to the south side of the street.

It was, the numbers indistinct against the peeling white paint. Three electric meters on the side said the large old place had been divided into apartments, but he saw the wide front porch with its swing still beckoned as if one family lived there. His father probably had leaned against the railing, watching the sky.

"God, it's like an old postcard, isn't it?" she said. He stood staring, hoping to feel something, again trying to force an image he'd never experienced, a memory he'd never had, of his father, of his unknown grandparents, of the equally unknown cousins, aunts, uncles, but nothing came except the here-and-now of an old house in a dying Nebraska town.

"Look," he said. "It's for sale. See the sign?"

"Why don't you buy it," she said. "Then you'd have something tangible. Isn't that what you want?"

Again, a flash of irritation in him, from her, but she was right to dismiss this like flotsam on someone else's sea. Just an old house. Sure, his father once had ridden a bicycle on that uneven sidewalk, and once the ice and milk wagons clacked down the cobbles to deliver to his grandmother. Once, he knew, there had been a once, at least for them. But for him surveying a dilapidated dwelling on a strange street in a strange town, well, it was like he'd felt on the Sahara. There wasn't any here, here, for him.

"Let's go," he said. They walked without conversation back to the car and in the motel they screwed with almost no sounds, desperately, as if flesh on flesh were an answer, not a question.

He awoke at three, her hot middle pressed against his thigh. What was that low, sireny whistle that awakened him? He strained to place it. Of course. The night wind rushing over the plains, over this low building, running eastward. A signal, he felt. He lifted himself gently from the bed. She stirred, rolled onto her other side. He kissed her shoulder. Then he pulled on his trousers and slipped into a black T-shirt. The Nikes went over bare feet. He closed the door with a soft click, and didn't start the LeBaron until he'd coasted away from their room door down the slope toward the motel office. Even this early an ochre knife-edge sat on the eastern horizon. He passed the outlying franchises: a Wal-Mart, a Pizza Hut, a Stop-N-Go, and then the car shuddered on the cobbles of Main Street.

At the intersection of Sixth Street, he started the westward turn. The Sears sign flared at him, suddenly huge and mocking, and he felt his eyes fill with salty water. Forty years ago he'd been there, just a boy, with spending money for the trip from Omaha, with the hearse housing his father, and while his mother negotiated with the monument maker just down the street, he'd bought a primitive electric drill to fix all that had gone wrong. But it hadn't worked, and his mother told him he was heartless to think of such a thing at such a time.

On Sixth, the headlights picked up the lawn ornaments and the eyes of cats left out for the night and the Big Wheels parked on the porches. At the dead end by the nursery, he turned north, then west at the sign. Two hundred yards further on he came to the cemetery gates, as wide open as the sky. He parked on the road around the curve from the caretaker's office. He took the flashlight from the glove box, and a half-pint of schnapps he always carried. The wind ripped at his clothes as he crunched the river gravel up toward the small outbuilding where they kept the records. He took a pull of schnapps, felt the sweet curl in his throat, a thick coil of heat sidling toward his brain. Mackerel-scale clouds scudded across the half-moon. The warm wind whistled over the old monuments and mausoleums. He stopped for a moment, looking west. They were somewhere in that middle section, he remembered. But where, precisely? Christ, he could remember his army serial number, and the telephone numbers of people in a dozen countries, and when he'd told his first lie, so why couldn't he recall where the graves were? He moved to the lee of the little office building. Fifty yards beyond he saw the caretaker's bungalow. No light, just the serenity of a home in the early morning hours. He tried the office's door. Locked. Now that was something, he thought, not to trust the dead. He tipped up the half-pint, stashed it in his hip pocket, then slid to the south window. With fingers under the mullions, he heaved upward. The sash moved with a squeak. He shoved the lower sash full open, hearing the weights bang in their channels. He forked his leg through, pulled his torso onto the sill until he felt his right leg touch the floor. Last came his left leg, with the dicey knee from softball played when he was too old for it.

The flashlight showed that the room held only a desk and a typewriter table. But on the desk lay the big records book. So long ago he'd filled out those forms, the data of the dead for the directory of the deceased. He moved the flashlight's beam to the book. The names and locations poured out in alphabetical columns: Anderson, Andrews, Arends, Berry, Buechler, Burnard, Cobb, Cogill, Collicott, Comstock, and then, his, Conaway. He traced his finger along the line. William J. Conaway. His name. His father's name. On the right edge, the plot's location, L-9. He moved his finger to the next line. Conover. But that shouldn't be, he nearly cried out, that shouldn't be, until he remembered that, no, his mother wouldn't be under Conaway. No, she'd had another name when she'd decided she'd had enough of mortality. He fished out the schnapps for a gulp, then flipped the pages although he knew she lay next to his father, that he'd insisted on that, that he'd find them together under his name. Maybe he just wanted to feel again the stinging shame of the other name. He found it: Lorraine C. Kohtz, L-9. C for Conaway, not her maiden name. At least she'd held onto the C.

He closed the book and turned to the wall map of plots. There, just down the center roadway to the L-marker, then left a few plots. He slipped the bottle and flashlight back into their pockets before swinging through the window. Carefully, he lowered the sash before scuttling across the driveway and onto the cemetery road. He noticed that the wind had laid a little with dawn approaching, but it still tossed the tree branches and ruffled what was left of his hair. He snapped on the flashlight, slowing his half-trot so that he could see slim white columns by the roadside marking the sections. He was at J. He felt his hard breathing, like a band around his chest. The soft life had done him in. Neither his father nor his mother ever gained an ounce, had walked everywhere, even near the end when his father's cancer ate him through. But with Mr. Kohtz his mother went soft as sin until she'd chosen the fast way of the razor over the slow way of the vodka. Another white shaft reared to his left. The light showed the deepcut black L. He turned onto the grassy avenue between the headstone rows that in the moonlight looked, in their different shapes and sizes, like some mutant plains crop, or the ranked remains of native idols.

He found the large stone first, between two evergreens. His light played over the chiselled letters spelling their names. Showers of brown needles washed out by the wind fell on and around him. Behind the big marker lay the smaller ones: Lorraine C. Kohtz,   1911-1960.   William J. Conaway, 1900-1950. The dates seemed deeper cut, as though more important. He now had lived longer than either of them had. An accident of fate. But he had lost their counsel early, never had their approval or disdain for his checkered adulthood. They had never seen their grandchildren. He glanced eastward at the brightening horizon, trying to blink back these tears. The sun seemed to be rising quickly, as if on a grandfather's clock calendar. Thick black clouds hung in a rope over its slender arc. He looked again at the carved names, and then he drained the schnapps, the liquid flowing into him and over his mouth, down his chin into droplets that fell in silver shards on the green grave-grass. Despite himself the tears fell, too, and he was kneeling between the stones murmuring what he thought might pass for prayers, or apologies. He knelt a long time, until the flashlight's beam was lost in the false dawn.

He stood then and walked to a sprinkler head. He filled the schnapps bottle. Next he went to a plot a few yards away. From the peony bush there he broke off two perfect white blossoms. He thrust their stems into the bottle's neck. At the plots, he put the bottle between the two small ones and stood looking down until a light blinked on in the caretaker's house. Then he walked back to his car. His eyes were clear, and he felt clean, guiltless.

He sat in the motel chair until nine-thirty, when he woke her with their old trick, the rattle of ice in a plastic cup filled with beer.

"Hi," she said. "Want to play?"

"Too late for me," he said. "I've been awake awhile."

"Oh," she said, and rolled out on the other side of the bed.

While she cleaned up, he packed, and after his shower, they drove into town for breakfast at the Big Red Café. This time she took the traditional route, ham and eggs and hash browns. He had thick white sausage gravy and biscuits, washed down with black coffee. After the waitress cleared their places, she looked directly at him, through him, it seemed.

"Well," she said, "isn't it time for the cemetery?"

He returned the look, seeing that her intuitive sensor, her warning system, was full on.

"No," he said, "what's dead is dead. Let's forget the past."

The sensor processed the words, and her eyes clouded in the apprehension.

"Surely," she said, "let's forget it."

They hardly spoke on the long drive back, and when they did it was of little things. The Last Chance, the wind and heat, the cobbled streets. She wore sunglasses all the way, even after dark, all the way into the city and to her apartment. He didn't help her to the door, but she only had her small suitcase. He didn't say he'd call her. He knew that she knew that tomorrow would be a day he needed to be with his wife and children, to check in on life, to let go of all that was at long last dead.

Corona Girl

I live alone, go out seldom, except to the only bar in town, Don Juan's. I go to Don Juan's bar because it's real, and nothing else is, I think. But maybe I see and feel things differently, askew, and that may owe to my prosthetic left leg, a Vietnam reminder, and no matter how good things may be, in the world's way, I know I'm walking a different way, just like most of the people at Don Juan's, whose lives seldom vary until someone like the Corona Girl comes along.

The problem is, we must wait for her, as we do for the buzzards that, like the swallows come to Capistrano, come each spring. We never know exactly when the Corona Girl is coming or what she will bring. So in the spring, we gather, not exactly awaiting her, but with the sense of anticipation, a tingling, that jingles our lives. We awaiters are several. Don Juan's offers equal opportunity waiting and frittering. I limp in from the gravel parking lot on a new-to-me spring-loaded leg. If I wanted I could hop in, jump high, all the way to the ceiling decorated with stamped-tin beer logos and banners from long-lost causes (although not Vietnam, more like the Chicago Cubs). I usually sit at the door end of the bar, next to the video-poker machines, not because I play video poker but because sitting there denies someone else the foolishness of playing it. I hate foolishness, like many here do. "'Nam" was foolish. Iraq, foolish. Hard-rock underground mining is foolish. Everything seems foolish except love, which is beyond foolishness.

In the bar, though, much of the talk is not about waiting or love, but about mining. This was a mining town. Hard rock. The levels ran from the mining center, San Isidro, twelve miles away, to this place. On rails, one level above the next, to the depth of 3,000 feet. Souvenir donkey engines and cars serve as outdoor art for the few businesses, including Don Juan's. When things are slack I go outside and sit on one of the engines. I feel like Gulliver amongst the Lilliputians. I'm so big on these engines. I watch the buzzards and the road, if it's Corona Girl season.

When I go back inside, I take my usual place by the video-poker machine even if someone has squatted there. I shake my artificial leg and holler how they should move because I can't move so well, and the person usually does, unless they're up from Tucson, all contemptuous, gawking at mountains and mines and locals, or unless they are drunk artisans from the local artists colony, who get unashamedly plowed every Saturday night. Dick the Prick is one of them. When he's drunk, which is often, he says if I were a real hero I would have lost both legs. This from a man who never served a day, so busy with his ceramic art that he got deferments. There were a lot of stone statues in 'Nam, but I never saw one made by him. I do remember one close by when the Bouncing Betty took my leg. A Buddha, I recall, always smiling. Then it was the tourniquet and the chopper and the base hospital and then Hawaii for a long time, and then back home, which I couldn't stand, too much pity and resentment and "did you kill any children, son?" from my mother. So I hid out here. I do landscaping, which isn't too hard in the desert, although it's hot work. I wear a Vietnamese rice-planter's hat, very wide brimmed, straw, and if I happen to catch glimpse of myself in a window reflection, would swear I was back there in a different body and soul.

That's where the Corona Girl really comes in, whoever she is this year. She's needed for this bunch. Aside from Dick the Prick, who accuses everyone of hitting on his imaginary girlfriend, the beautiful, heavily tattooed Shirley (who's married with three kids) or of alienating the locals (ironic since he's a transplant like me), the roster reads pretty good. At the long bar there were almost always Al and Al, a.k.a. Aloysius and Alice, both retired and good-natured, but with a sad air about them owing to Alice's breast cancer. At the end were the Smiths, father and son. Old Smithy had spent thirty-six years underground and it hadn't helped his mood, which ranged from cranky to mean. He took it out on his son, Clarence, who at nearly forty went about with a genetic snarl, muttering that his father was a brute and he couldn't wait to get out of town, which he hadn't done, ever. Across from the long bar and the two shorter bars, you could almost always find Joe the Engineer, one of the last people still employed at the Alhambra Mine. He drove real railroad engines from the Alhambra to the Sizzle Mine, forty miles away, with what little ore worth smelting could still be extracted from the Alhambra. His ambition was to steal the Alhambra's three remaining locomotives and drive them around a curve at high speed so they'd wreck. "That'd teach the sons of bitches," he'd say. In his off time, Joe fixed automobiles, at least those without on-board computers.

Next to Joe perched the Wacko Brothers, twins with 'Nam disease like me. They drank their pitchers, played a little pool watching the buzzards out the big terrace doors, and often sat with that thousand-yard stare, looking at one another or Shirley bustling around the bar. They listened to '70s rock, of which Don Juan's jukebox had a plenitude. Both Tim and Jim, that was their names, had failing lungs. "Either the Agent Orange or the mine," one or the other would say, then shrug in unison and hoist a mug. They often entertained the Indians, as the Don Juan folks called them, meaning Native Americans who used to chop and load ore, and the Mexicans, who did the same. Foremost among these was the Bandit, a Mexican-American of great size and good will, married to a twig of an Anglo who must have spent most of her conjugal time on top, lest she be squashed. When things got out of hand, as they sometimes did at Don Juan's, if the Bandit was there he put a stop to it, if necessary with a pool cue, as he did when four wannabe Hell's Angels motored up from Tucson to imitate Brando's *The Wild One*, bringing false bravado to a place where the bravado was real. They swaggered in, ordered too much to drink, hassled Shirley, took over the pool table and the jukebox (they actually liked Barry Manilow) and started bad-mouthing the place, the town, us.

"Bunch of crips and dicks," one said. "Been underground too long," another added. "Haven't gone down enough," the third said, which was when Shirley swatted the last one with a bar towel and called him a ferret-faced little asshole. He tried to slap her, but Shirley ducked and went for the loaded blackjack under the bar. But Dick the Prick quickly took issue and when they ganged on him, the Bandit started bashing with a cue, joined by the Wacko Twins and even Al and Al, the latter of whom swung a mean beer bottle. By the time the Sheriff's folks arrived, things were pretty quiet, except for the moans. Me, I just tripped two, easy to do with a metal leg, as is stomping. That and sneak out to pour Equal from the bar into their gas tanks. The cops wrote them up and told them to be good. Just then the Corona Girl's van pulled in. I was lucky, being outside sugaring the biker's rides. This Corona Girl had an escort, who opened Don Juan's door for her. I heard her call him Ben. He was razor thin and jerky-hard, and he ushered her inside like she was a princess. She carried a papier-mâché parrot like the one in the Corona TV ads, except this figment recorded and played back sounds, as I found when the bar-babble came out of the bird and later on, stuff that I don't think anybody wanted to hear twice. I followed the entrance as closely as I could, beguiled by her youth, twenty-two at the most, and pretty in the way Elizabeth Taylor once was. The Corona Girl wore short-shorts and a Corona T-shirt tied above her belly button. As soon as she entered, the remains of the mêlée ceased. Dick the Prick went to gargle. The battered bikers wiped their faces on their sleeves. Or forearms. The Vs went back to their drinks. Shirley put on a smile. The 'Nam brothers tried not to look at her. Joe turned away, anxious not to be seen admiring her van, visible from the buzzard-watching patio. Paul the resident poet, from his post at the far end of the bar, gaped as if trying to make mental notes for a sonnet. First thing was, though, that Ben, who'd carried a hamper in, took a few double sawbucks out and gave them to Shirley. Then Corona Girl jumped on the bar. She cried out, "Free, free Coronas for everyone. Belly up."

Everyone did, in a sort of stampede, except me. I was already bellied up. The first thing the mechanical parrot said was, "Fuck me," which I think had emanated from Paul the Poet, distracted for a moment from his dispensation to be taken seriously. Paul, whom I deeply liked, was given to declamations, owing to an artistic personality driven by age, fear, and booze. From the end of the bar, Ben began handing out trinkets, much applauded by us Don Juansians. It was then from my position at the outermost part of the bar that I saw Corona Girl was luminescent. She brought it in from outside, light-stick necklaces that glowed blue in the dark bar. She went from drinker to drinker draping them about our necks, even of the three dogs that hung out here: Paz de la Paz, Cheerio, and Dubious. The dogs took them as if they were sacramental. So did the rest of us. I stroked mine, hoping it would turn to gold. The 'Nam twins whirled theirs, as if fetching something from the air. Paul the Poet at first disdained his but then convinced himself it was a talisman. Shirley laughed, put on four, and then snatched a souvenir hat for herself. Dick the Prick even relented and took a necklace saying if it was good enough for his dog it was good enough for him. I agreed. Throughout this, there descended a strange calm, not quiet because we were all talking, but calm, as if the edges had worn off things. Closest thing I ever had to it was a listening post on the Ho Chi Minh Trail, when there was absolute silence. I once asked one of the Wacko Brothers about it, and he said, "It's God taking a break, then shit'll break loose."

Anyway, Corona Girl lit up the place: those glowy things, hats, T-shirts, free beer, all the money the jukebox could hold. Even the Tucson bikers dropped their faux-tough shit and did little jigs when Van Morrison came on. They looked almost human. Then about the fourth free Corona, the Corona Girl hoisted herself onto the bar and began to dance. Strangely, Ben just watched and whistled the tune, I think it was "Hotel California." She danced, in the words of the Guy Clark song, "like no one was watching." The calm descended to silence until she was finished. She threw the last trinkets out, bottle openers and fridge magnets, like she was on a Mardi Gras float. Applause broke out led by Paul the Poet who kept shouting "Bravo" like this was an operatic show. Finally, Corona Girl got off the bar, waving, and still tossing things to the barflies, her eyes, though, showing the little stress lines that come with fatigue and knowing you're not doing what you should be doing. I was studying that in the moment after she descended, when the prophesied shit broke loose.

The drunkest surviving biker gave out a sort of Rebel yell and charged the bar shouting, "Corona is Life." He vaulted it, landing to Shirley's side, grabbed a bottle of tequila, threw back several gulps, backhanded Shirley, vaulted back and ran for the pool table and the outside terrace. The Bandit managed to cue-trip him at the big French doors, and so, shaved head first, the biker crashed through the glass, tumbled twice, and rolled over the low terrace wall, right into the base of the buzzard tree. The birds were quicker than we were. By the time any of us got to the unconscious biker, they'd already started flapping around him. We shooed them. Shirley, wiping tears, called the Sheriff, who brought the list of names he'd taken on his first visit, and said he sure hoped Don Juan's wouldn't become a desired destination point for half-assed punks from Tucson. I wasn't at the Buzzard fête, not being so mobile. I did see Corona Girl hug Shirley. Then Ben put his big arms around Corona Girl's shoulders, now slumped, and took her out to the van. They were gone by the time the fire department's EMT van got there for the biker, and the Sheriff asked a few questions. I thought, while finishing my beer, that this had been an odd evening, the oddest since my last sexual encounter, when my partner, an elementary school teacher from San Isidro, stuck a fridge magnet on my leg and licked cocaine off it.

The rest of us clientele sort of hung around, drinking and retelling the story. Al and Al finally bought a bar bottle and left without a word. Paul the Poet said he thought he could use this. The 'Nam brothers opined that they should have left that guy for the buzzards, while Dick the Prick nodded, adding that they could have set the dogs on him. The Smiths, who'd stayed at the bar through it all, just quaffed, although Clarence did say he wouldn't have minded taking them bikers out to Rattlesnake Rock and by God if any more came in he'd sure do that. Joe the Engineer proclaimed that running them over with a big diesel would show them. Lots of chaff drifted in the air, like when the helicopters came in close and dumped aluminum chips to divert the SAMS. We were all still wearing the stick-light necklaces, even the dogs, and twilight had set so we all glowed blue, as if we were ghosts. Nobody mentioned that Corona Girl had gone. Nobody had to. The air had gone out of the room. We lingered a bit, then drifted away to our private sorrows, and that was the end of Corona Girl night at Don Juan's.

But it wasn't, not for me. A few weeks later I was in Tucson for a checkup at the VA. Part of my in-town ritual involved a good Mexican meal, and old-fashioned as it is, I like El Charro. I park in the handicapped space and then walk the downtown district, just to kill time, as though you could kill time, God be praised. Anyway, I saw our Corona Girl and Ben coming out of a gallery in their party regalia. Both seemed too tired to live. I would have approached, but nobody needs a gimpy reacquaintance. Ben treated her as tenderly as before. I turned away and ate a good meal. I didn't see our special Corona Girl until yet another few weeks later, when I again went to Tucson and saw her in a Target store. She still seemed to me to be cloaked in blue light. She pushed a shopping cart with two small kids in it, one boy, one girl. Ben wasn't around. I tried to stay anonymous, but she saw me and waved, a dainty one-hand wave, and then went forward to the diapers section. I never saw her again. I imagine her someplace safe and rich, surrounded by the light-stick light, embraced by Ben and Shirley and all of us in absentia. No good, of course, like wishing beyond hope all future Corona Girls would be like her, or for my phantom leg to become real, but wishing gets me through the night. My dog Dubious still glows.

James McKinley is the author of four previous books. His work has appeared in *Esquire*, *Playboy*, *StoryQuarterly*, and elsewhere. For many years, he edited *New Letters* at the University of Missouri-Kansas City, where he also directed the Professional Writing Program and co-founded two annual writing conferences. His honors include two MacDowell Colony fellowships and senior Fulbright lectureships to Yugoslavia, Hungary, and Spain, and he is a past board president of the Associated Writing Programs. He lives in Kansas City and in Oracle, Arizona.